THE
RISE AND RISE
TABITHA BAIRD

Arabella Weir is an actress, comedian and writer best known for *The Fast Show*. She makes regular appearances on TV and radio and is a frequent contributor to national newspapers. She has written several books for adults including the international bestseller, *Does My Bum Look Big in This?*

This is her first book for children. She lives in North London with her two teenagers and maybe a dog . . . soon.

THE
RISE AND RISE
OF TABITHA BAIRD

ARABELLA WEIR

Piccadilly

First published in Great Britain in 2014
by Piccadilly Press
Northburgh House, 10 Northburgh Street,
London, EC1V 0AT

www.piccadillypress.co.uk

A CIP catalogue record for this book is available from the British Library.

ISBN: 978-1-84812-419-6

1 3 5 7 9 10 8 6 4 2

Printed and bound by Clays Ltd, St Ives Plc

Piccadilly Press is part of the Bonnier Publishing Group
www.bonnierpublishing.com

For my own teenagers, Isabella and Archie,
with all my love

SUMMER TERM WEEK 1

THE EVENING BEFORE SCHOOL STARTS...

Ohgodohgodohgodohgodohgod, I feel sick. Tomorrow's my first day at the new school, Heathside Academy, and the school skirt looks really, really, *reeeeeally* bad on me. It didn't look like this last week.

I tried it on three days in a row AND two of those times were after I'd eaten. You know how some things look different on you after you've eaten? And the skirt did look okay. Obvs, it didn't look brilliant or designery or anything nice. How could it, it's school uniform, duh? But, you know, it did look normal. Now it looks like a blooming kilt, all bunched up and too materialy. I can't face walking into the new school wearing this. I might as well wear a massive sign around my neck, like homeless people sometimes do, but instead of it saying:

PLEASE GIVE ME 50P
FOR A CUP OF TEA

mine would say,

HELLO,
I'M NEW HERE.
HAVE YOU NOTICED HOW ENORMOUS
I LOOK IN THIS HORRIBLE SKIRT?

The skirt makes me look super-fat and I really, really, really don't want to start my new school as THE SUPER-FAT ONE. I know I'm not actually, in real life, SUPER-FAT, like kids in documentaries who are so huge their parents send them away to be slimmed down by defatting experts in special camps, usually in America. The kids all live in wooden huts, crying while they're made to eat lettuce by someone wearing shorts and shouting at them. Then later they sneak about in the dark plotting to get out and eat chocolate and hamburgers (not at the same time, obvs). But in this skirt, I actually do look THAT fat!

I am a bit fat, though, I s'pose. How could I forget? Mum is *always* going on about it, calling me her 'roly-poly' and I know that's just another way of saying 'fatty'. She thinks if she makes her snide remarks 'amusing' (they never are) then it doesn't count as badgering me. She says things like, 'Should you really be eating peanut butter and jam, my podgy little pudding?' and, 'Maybe push yourself away from the table, rather than drag yourself towards it, for a change, angel?' And her hilarious favourite, always said in that I'm-not-being-horrible-but-I've-just-noticed-this-interesting-fact voice that makes me want to scream, 'Oh, by the way, my darling girl, have you heard – chocolate is fattening?'

EAT ME

CHOCOLATE
BISCUITS

Anyway, I can't think about Mum's pathetic, non-stop attempts to give me an eating disorder right now. I've got to work out what to do with the skirt. I've tried rolling it over a few times, but that makes the skirty bit stick right out like a ballet tutu. I've tried it on back to front and that's a bit better, but there are buttons down the front and they look a bit weird on the back. I don't want anyone to notice me.

Well, actually, that's not true – I mean, I don't want them to notice me for the wrong reasons, and looking fat and stupid in my skirt is definitely the wrongest of reasons.

At least it's not a second-hand skirt. Mum seriously, not-even-trying-to-be-funny suggested getting me a second-hand skirt from the school shop! She kept going on about how short we are of money now, and how because I always rolled the top of my last school skirt over, I was probably going to do the same thing with this one, and that by the time I'd rolled it over to make it short no one would know it was second-hand!

I told her I would literally kill myself and then never talk to her ever again if I had to wear a second-hand skirt, and then she accused me of not caring about her situation and how awful it all was for her.

Typical Mum. Of course, she has no idea that I *do* know all about how she feels from reading her blog! But, you know, you'd think a proper mum might worry more about how her kids were doing and how they were coping instead of always talking about *her* feelings.

In the end Gran bought the skirt cos I think maybe Mum really doesn't have any money now.

It's a whole week since Mum, Luke and I left Ivy House for the last time ever – the house Luke and I were born and brought up in. I felt really sad but really excited too. Yay! We've moved in with Gran (Mum's mum). Okay, not-so-yay, but it's great to be in London, near shops and cinemas, and I won't have to spend lots of time with my know-it-all, swotty-Horace, lame, ten-year-old brother Luke just because we live in the middle of nowhere and there's no one else around.

Anyway, I didn't want to stay in Bankside Marsh, Middle-of-Nowhereshire because we'd have had to move to a much smaller house but in the same village, and we'd end up living near Dad but not with him any more. It would be so horrible, seeing our old house taken over by a new family who are probably all happy and fine and will stay there forever because they don't have a drunk dad who ruins everything.

And if we stayed I might see girls from my old school, Greyfriars Ladies' College, who all know that I had to leave because we can't afford the fees any more, and they'd pity me. The shame would be unbearable – and anyway I didn't actually like Greyfriars. It was just filled with stupid, super-thin girls who are good at sports and get fake tans and watch *Made in Chelsea* and think I'm not as pretty as them.

On my last day of school all the girls gathered round, supposedly to say goodbye, but really they were being snooty and catty, saying things like, 'Oh my god, you're going to a comprehensive school, poor you. I *sooooo* totes could not do that,' and 'I feel *sooooo* sorry for you, Tabitha, you won't get a proper education now. Oh my god, maybe you'll end up working in a shop or something *troooooly* dreadful like that.'

The worst was from that totally lame, not-nearly-as-gorgeous-as-she-thinks-she-is Olivia, who said, 'You'll probably get some awful diseases from the other kids at a place like that.'

I could have killed them.

I'm nervous enough about starting a new school in the middle of the year. I don't need them all giving me their brilliant ideas about what happens at an 'ordinary' school, which is what Miss Peak called it when she said goodbye. I won't catch diseases, will I?

I never really fitted in at Greyfriars. S'pose I didn't try to either. Our family was too poor and never 'quite right'. Most of the girls there came from families that owned big estates or huge farms or their dads worked for some big bank. They were all called things like Pandora and Aurora and Plethora. Everyone knew we weren't really proper rich – we weren't, even before Dad lost what we did have.

Now Dad's going to live with his mum, Gran Baird, or GB as we call her, which she does *not* like because, she says, it makes her sound like a country. We started calling her GB when we were little, because she was so posh and different to Mum's mum, who was always just like an ordinary gran.

It's really embarrassing – your dad living with his mum when he's forty-six years old. I'm not going to tell anyone at my new school that's where he lives . . . I'll say he works abroad or something.

Dad didn't even come to wave us off like he promised. Big surprise. Soooo unlike Dad not to do something he promised to do. Hah, hah. He sent me a text saying, *Please don't be cross with Daddy for not waving you all off. I couldn't, it would have made me too sad.*

Hmm. Which means he probably felt less sad in the pub.

When he says or texts things like that I feel like

texting back, *Why shouldn't you be sad? I'm sad and it's all your fault*, but then I never do. I don't know why – I suppose there's no point and I sort of feel sorry for him too. I wish I didn't, because it *is* all his fault.

So, we've finally, actually, for-real moved into Gran's house. It smells a bit of cats, which is a bit random cos Gran doesn't have a cat. Gran has Basil, and he is so not a cat. Basil is Gran's dog but she reckons he's her son!

He's all right and doesn't smell. Not that Gran would mind if he did. She loves him so much he's allowed to do whatever he likes. Gran treats Basil the way GB treats Dad and the way Mum treats Luke – all spoilt boys!

Gran's given me the bedroom on the first floor by the bathroom. It's pretty great because I'm nowhere near Mum or Luke. They're on the top floor, next to each other, of course, because Mum adores him and he's her favourite. How perfect for them that they're literally neighbours. (Can you say neighbours when it's *inside* a house?)

I feel a bit weird moving in here, though. I love Gran. She can be really funny and isn't like an old lady at all, but her house is much, much smaller than Ivy House and moving in here feels like we're letting the whole world know we're not doing very well.

When I have to tell people that I live with my mum AND my gran (and my brother, worse luck) it's definitely going to feel like I've got a T-shirt on, or something, that says *MY FAMILY ARE POOR*.

I don't suppose I have to tell people at my new school where we used to live or where I went to school. And it's not like we were super-rich – not like all those others girls at Greyfriars. Their houses were all so enormous they made even Ivy House look like a doll's house! I suppose, maybe, what I mean is, that it's all different now. Before, at least we looked more like a normal family . . . even if only, as it turned out, from the outside.

I hope not everyone at the new school lives with their mum and dad, all happy families and everything. Oh god, what if they're not that, but instead they're all clinically or morbidly obese (or whatever it's called when someone's so huge they start talking about them on the news), or living off benefits (I don't even know what 'off benefits' means), or drug addicts with knives and they're infested with horrible infectious illnesses like everyone at Greyfriars is convinced they'll be?

I've decided I am not going to be an outsider at this place. I am going to fit in. No more, 'Ah, poor Tabitha, she doesn't have her own pony and her dad's an alky'. Make way for, 'Hey, Tabitha . . . lovin' that . . . ' (Erm, can't think of anything super-cool right now.) 'You're rocking.' I am going to be super five-star popular at my new school for definite. Yup, that is what I'm going to be now.

By the way, if I am happy and popular at this school, I hereby solemnly swear to do a good person job when I'm older. You know, a job like a nurse or a doctor or a dental assistant – one of those yucky jobs where you have to deal with other people's gross things like boils and warts and stinky tongues. Jobs really caring, nice people do.

SUMMER TERM WEEK 1

MONDAY
(FIRST DAY OF SCHOOL!!)

School was great! I LOVE IT!!!!! All right, I don't want to sound too keen or that it was the best day of my life or anything saddo like that, and obviously it's school so it's impossible to love, love, love it, but it was *soooooo* different from Greyfriars. Completely, totally, in-every-way different. For starters, there are boys there. Not that I'm interested in them. I don't even like them – pathetic losers – but it is very cool to be at a mixed school. So much cooler than the 'ladies' college' that Greyfriars liked to call itself!

I sorted the skirt by cutting off the waistband, so that it is less bulky. Mum is literally going to kill me if she ever finds out. I am a genius – it really worked. All the too-materialy bit was in the waistband, it turned out. Anyway, I cut it off with Gran's patchwork-making scissors (sharp!), and I rolled the top of the skirt over, like I always did with the Greyfriars one, but then it kept slipping down – turns out the waistband is there to hold the skirt up. That must be why they put them on trousers, too – to stop them falling down. But, no prob, I got one of Luke's belts (Wrangler, just how uncool can he be?!) and put that on over the outside, leaving a bit of the skirt hanging over the top and then folded that bit down over and under the belt. It looked really cool that way.

It must have looked good because the first person to speak to me at Heathside Academy, which I've already found out everyone calls HAC (glad I learnt that on the first day) was this really pretty girl, A'isha. She came up to me and said, 'How do you get your skirt to look all flat like that and not bunched up?'

I was so relieved. It was great someone actually started a conversation. I told her what I'd done and she was really impressed. A'isha was wearing a plain, dark scarf thing over her head which completely covered her hair and was pinned together under her chin, so you could only see her face. There was this horrible moment when I just knew she was looking at me like I was looking at her and thinking her scarf thing was a bit weird. I wasn't actually thinking that at all – I'd just never seen a girl my age wearing one. There was not one even remotely not-completely-pink girl at Greyfriars. That's another great thing about HAC – there aren't just boys, there are so many different types of kids. Loads of girls wearing scarves like A'isha's too.

Luckily A'isha didn't take offence. She just said, 'It's called a hijab. My dad makes me wear it.' And then she rolled her eyes and made a really funny what-a-loser face which made me laugh out loud.

Apparently her dad's a Muslim and is all serious about the hijab when she tries to go out to school or wherever without it on, but doesn't mind that she wants to go to university and mixes with boys all day. She said, laughing, that she calls it 'Messed-up Muslim.'

A'isha was really nice. I think she's one of the cool kids here because practically everyone who passed us while we were talking nodded at her and she nodded back, but without anyone saying anything. As far as I can tell, that's what they do here – just nod at each other. They don't do completely awks 'hellos' or anything, just a really tiny nod of the head. It's *sooooo* cool.

I think A'isha and I are going to be proper friends. I could die of gratitude. So, I've got one friend now, so just one (or maybe two?) more to get – fingers crossed.

When I got home, Mum had loads of questions. She used to go to Heathside Academy years ago, before it was an Academy, though. Whenever we visited Gran she always used to point in the direction of its huge glass and wood building – about ten times the size of Greyfriars – set back from the road, with a strip of scrappy, faded grass in front of it, and remind us she went there.

In fact, as I left this morning she said, 'Hope they don't remember me, or you've got no chance!'

I didn't bother to tell her that as she changed her name when she got married, no one was going to realise I'm her daughter, and I'm certainly not going to mention it! And anyway, she was there a trillion years ago. Mum is absolutely ancient – forty-one years old! All her teachers will have been dead for years.

As long as I've got anything to do with it, Mum isn't even going to set foot in my new school – no thank you. I'm not having her telling teachers – or worse, other parents – about her marriage break-up and that embarrassing 'healing-process' blog she's started where she blabs on and on about it all.

SUMMER TERM
WEEK 1
TUESDAY

It **was only** the second day of my new school, don't forget, so today was quite important! I was a tiny, weeny bit less nervous than yesterday and I'd managed to get my skirt looking exactly like it did then, so that helped.

I looked for A'isha immediately I got to school but couldn't see her, which was okay, but, you know, it would have been cool to walk into class with her.

I'd practised a few times last night what I was going to say when I saw her and decided not to act too keen – nobody wants to be mates with someone they think is desperate to be their friend. I don't want her to think

I'm a loser with no mates. Okay, so it's true, I don't actually have any friends yet, not here, not now we've left Bankside Marsh and come to live with Gran. But I wouldn't have said I had any real friends back there, just pretentious pretend-friends. I am going to make proper friends here at HAC, friends forever, friends who will like me for who I am.

Anyway, I'd decided if/when I saw A'isha I'd say, 'Oh hi, you all right?' and not, 'Can we have lunch together?' because although that is what I really, really wanted to know, I decided I couldn't ask that the moment I first clapped eyes on her because of not-looking-desperate.

Obviously I couldn't hang around waiting to spot her all day so I decided to head straight for my class. But then I realised I'd forgotten where our classroom was.

I walked up the huge concrete central staircase, which I definitely remembered doing yesterday, and then panicked when I got to the second floor. I knew my classroom wasn't on the first floor because A'isha had pointed out a huge, really ill-looking plant at the end of the first-floor corridor. She said everyone called it The Trainer, after one of the PE teachers who apparently looks like that plant. He or she must be pretty weird-looking.

Anyway, I wrongly decided that it was the right floor and walked straight into what I thought must be our classroom. I couldn't be sure because the door looked exactly like all the other doors. The ENTIRE ROOM was full of kids much older than me – definitely fifteen plus – who all turned and stared at me at the same time.

I just froze. The expressions on their faces were as if I was drooling or my hair was on fire or I was topless or something. It felt like a billion years of me just standing there with them all gawping at me before I realised it actually wasn't my classroom. Oh god, now every single person from that class is going to think I'm a complete idiot and realise that I'm new to the school too. It was horrible! I just stood there and they just stared at me.

I wanted to ask where my class was but my mouth,

as if by magic, instantly went bone-dry and I just couldn't get a single word out. I must have looked like a total moron. I tried to speak but my tongue just stuck to the roof of my mouth like it was the Sahara Desert in there.

Then a teacher walked into the room and had to push past me, as I was frozen to the spot (even though it felt like I was on fire!) She asked what my name and form were and I couldn't answer because of my tongue being stuck to the roof of my mouth.

Eventually, I managed to speak, and instead of 'Tabitha', all I got out was 'Tap'. I said my name was Tap! I told her my name was something from a sink! I didn't mean to say Tap, obviously, I meant to say Tabitha, but somehow all that came out was the first bit Tab . . . and it didn't sound like Tab, it definitely sounded like I'd said Tap!

I think I heard a few of them laugh, but the teacher shushed them, looked at me with her eyes wide open and repeated 'Tap?' in a tone of voice that was obviously meant to sound like she was in charge but, to me, sounded like she thought I was taking the mick.

I didn't know what to do. In the end I was just so

desperate to get away I shook my head, ran out and closed the door quickly behind me. Then I really did hear the whole class burst into laughter. I just wanted to die. I couldn't believe I'd managed to walk into the completely wrong class AND then get my own name wrong. *My own name.* I've never said my own name wrong. Who says their own name wrong? I could have said 'Tab', which at least is short for Tabitha.

Brainwave – I'm going to call myself Tab (not Tap, obvs). It's much cooler than Tabitha, and then hopefully everyone will just think they misheard my name. Tap isn't that different to Tab, is it?

Mum and Dad hate anyone calling me Tab. 'We've given you the beautiful name of Tabitha, which means gazelle, and you've shortened it to something that sounds like an option on a keyboard.' (BTW I've seen pictures of me as a baby and I couldn't have looked less like a girl who was going to end up being gazelle-like than if I'd been an actual watermelon.)

EPIC WATERMELON BABY

I stood in the corridor, with still no idea where my class was and now wanting to cry, which I knew I couldn't do. Imagine being caught crying straight after saying your name was Tap — the first thing anyone with a brain would say would be, 'Oh, I see, you're a *leaky* tap!'

But then one good, really good, thing happened. This girl ran past me and suddenly stopped, turned back and said, 'Aren't you the new girl in my class?'

I didn't recognise her so I just said, 'Erm?' and she said, 'Yeah, come on, hurry up, we're late'.

I was so grateful I nearly jumped for joy, and how uncool would that have been?

While we were running up the stairs (turns out our classroom is on the third floor, duh!) she said her name was Emz (she spelt it for me — cool spelling), short for Emma, and her parents hate it, just like mine hate Tab.

We got to the class at exactly the same time as the teacher was walking in, and although she did give us a bit of a sarky look, we weren't technically late so Miss couldn't say anything, so that was brilliant.

CHOCOLATE
BISCUITS

At lunch break I went into the canteen to eat my packed lunch – Mum is making me take one in every day. She said I can't have school lunches cos they're too expensive. They're like two or three pounds – we can't be that poor! But Mum says we are.

It was mobbed. It looked like the whole entire school was in there. I couldn't see A'isha in the crowds, and I didn't know if she'd invite me to sit at her table anyway if I did see her, so I just sat at the first empty seat I spotted.

I was sitting on my own, which was super embarrassing, especially if anyone who'd seen me call myself Tap had noticed me. I just stared at my sandwich, like a couple of pieces of bread and filling were the most interesting thing in the world, you know, so that I wouldn't catch anyone's eye. And then Emz walked right up, just like that, and said, 'Shall I join you or can't you bear to be torn away from that sandwich that you're so madly in love with?'

She was smiling when she said it so I knew straightaway she was joking and not being horrible. I was so pleased she'd come up – it was the second time that day she'd saved me.

We chatted away. She's an only-child and actually said about herself, 'I'm your classic spoilt only-child. I can get my parents to buy me anything I want – they are so pathetic, a right pair of pushovers.' She was laughing when she told me this, so I don't think she thinks they really are pathetic.

Lucky her, though, eh? How weird to have parents that will let you have anything you want.

And then, out of nowhere, A'isha came up and said, 'So, your real name's Tap, is it?'

I didn't know what to say. Emz looked at A'isha like she didn't understand what was going on, and then at me as if I should explain. I had some sandwich in my mouth at the time, so I couldn't say anything immediately. I just sort of froze again, and even after the bit of sandwich had gone down I couldn't think of what to say.

I didn't want to tell them the whole story – it was so awful, I thought they might start teasing me. I just looked down at my sandwich. Then A'isha, plonking herself down at the table, said, 'I heard what happened when you barged into 11E — only the baddest-teacher -in-school's class. Hmm, nifty move for a newbie! Did you hear what she did, Emz?' And then A'isha told her the story.

Emz started laughing and I suddenly realised they both thought I'd told the teacher my name was Tap *on purpose* to annoy her! And even though I hadn't, it felt really good that they were laughing at something I'd done.

This is so great! They think I'm funny even though I wasn't actually trying to be funny. I used to try to be funny back at Greyfriars and sometimes the other girls did laugh and stuff but it was so strict at that place that if one of the teachers there had ever thought I was being cheeky I'd have been sent to the headmistress straight away.

It's brilliant – turns out Emz and A'isha are already best mates (which has got to mean Emz is as cool as A'isha, doesn't it?) and now they think I'm the sort of cool girl who is cheeky to teachers!

I'm definitely going to think something else up to do on purpose next time. It can't be too naughty – I don't want to end up getting excluded! I could just do some of the stuff I do to Mum that winds her up so much, like pretending I can't hear her when she's asking me to do something, or that I don't understand certain words that I actually do understand so she has to explain them again and again and then I pretend I still don't get it.

Ooh, that'd be a really easy one to do in class – ask the teacher what something means and then just keep saying, 'I don't understand, can you explain it again, Miss?' I'd have to be careful not to end up looking like a moron, but I'm sure I can come up with something.

Mum's always moaning about me on her blog – it's got some name she thinks is funny but really is just depressing. Mum actually wrote a whole long thing about how her daughter (me!!) didn't understand anything and was asking advice from her readers if she should take me for a hearing test or some sort of IQ test. It was hilarious! Mum thinks I ask her things over and over again because I might be backward or slightly hard of hearing! I get brilliant ideas for how to wind Mum up just by reading her blog – if only she knew!

Oh, man! (I got that off A'isha. She says, 'Oh, man,' before she says practically everything. I like it much better than, 'Oh, god,' or, 'OMG', but we still say those too. 'Oh, man,' sounds really, really cool and a bit American high schooly.) Anyway . . . oh man, today was COMPLETELY AND TOTALLY BRILLIANT.

Emz and A'isha were already sitting at a table together in class when I walked in. I didn't think I could just walk over and plonk myself down with them like I was all, 'Take it as read that I assume you've now let me into your twosome and I'm just going to sit with you two forever.' They might have given me horrible looks, like, 'What the hell are you doing sitting down at our table? We didn't invite you. Just because we had lunch with you doesn't mean we're bezzies all of a sudden.'

I felt a bit panicky, and didn't know what to do. I looked around to see where else there was to sit, but then, thank god, they immediately both beckoned me over, completely naturally and matey, like they meant it.

I was *soooo* pleased . . . and relieved. I don't know what I'd have done if they had ignored me.

There *is* another girl, Grace, who's smiled at me and, on the first day, without me asking her to, showed me where the loos were when I was desperate to go and couldn't find them. But she's a bit, I don't know, geeky. It's like she is deliberately trying to look geeky. She always wears her school cardigan done up — all the buttons — and she wears the skirt at the proper length and absolutely no one here does that as far as I can tell so far. Her hair is cut like a dolly's, with a big, chunky fringe — it looks like someone put a pudding bowl on her head and then cut around that with a pair of garden shears. And she wears a hairband. A hairband?! Who wears a hairband? It's not even to keep her fringe off her face, which I suppose I could understand. She wears it behind her fringe as an accessory, like she means it. Even the worst proper-pony girls at Greyfriars didn't wear hairbands.

I don't think Grace has got many friends. I haven't seen her with anyone in particular yet. I doubt anyone who wears a hairband, if they're under sixty, has many friends.

I'm glad she showed me where the loos were, and didn't laugh at me for being new and not knowing, but I am not going to make friends with her just because of that. I won't be horrible to her or anything, but if I am going to be cool here then I need cool friends, obvs, and cool people do not wear hairbands. End of.

Today, second lesson, we were supposed to have ethics, culture and society (it was called religious education at Greyfriars, which is a bit clearer, I think, but this is supposed to be more 'inclusive of all cultures . . .' whatever that means!) but the teacher, Mr Long (hah, hah, apparently he's actually quite short) was not in, so we had a supply teacher called Mr Oliver.

He walked into our class and was all bossy and strict even before we'd got our books out. He barked, 'Right, I won't stand for any mucking about. Today we're looking at Islam.' So, A'isha puts her hand up and said, 'Sir, I'm a Muslim,' which made a few people in the class snigger a bit.

A'isha gave them a sort of shut-up look but you could see she wasn't being really serious because she knows everyone knows she's not really that Muslimy. She eats sausages when she's round other people's houses and only wears the headscarf because of her dad (and because it means she doesn't have to wash her hair every day, she told me.)

Mr Oliver looked a bit confused by this, as if he hadn't expected anyone to know anything about anything until he'd told us.

I hate it when teachers think only they know anything about anything and we kids, their pupils, are like empty bucket-brains waiting to be filled up by their genius! Just like Luke!

And then he asked, like he was testing her, which I suppose he was, 'Okay, perhaps you can help us out then – which country has the largest population of Muslims?'

The whole class went silent. We all knew this wasn't really a proper learning-about-Islam question. It was more of a I-know-more-than-you-know-even-though-you're-a-Muslim type of question. Poor A'isha looked like she didn't have a clue. But I did! Amazingly, I knew the answer! It had been a question on some nerd's game that Luke (of course) had been playing with Mum, and she'd been super impressed because he'd known the answer.

'Indonesia!' I called out, without putting my hand up.

Mr Oliver looked at me, surprised. So did everyone else. He said, 'That's right, well done, er . . . what's your name?'

Now, I don't actually know why I did this and I

definitely hadn't planned to, but because I thought he'd been a bit mean to A'isha and I wanted to pay him back, I said, 'It's Tap, sir. My name is Tap.'

I could feel the whole class looking at me like they were thinking, 'What are you doing?' and I saw Emz and A'isha look at each other and smile. It felt brilliant.

Mr Oliver screwed his eyes up really tight and looked at me so hard I thought I'd blurt out the truth right there, immediately.

'Your name is Tap?'

'Yes, sir, Tap.'

'Your parents gave you the name of a kitchen appliance, Tap?' he sneered. The more he looked and sounded like he knew I was taking the mick, the stronger I felt I had to keep the joke going. I couldn't really back down there and then, could I? I mean, once you've started you've sort of got to keep going, otherwise you'd lose face and everyone would know you were completely chicken.

And then it came to me – I said in my most super-innocent golly-gosh-Pony-Club voice, 'Yes, sir, they chose that name because my dad's a plumber.'

At that the whole class whooped and laughed really

hard and some boys even banged their tables with their fists. I felt scared but excited at the same time. I was scared that Mr Oliver was going to know I was making this all up and punish me, but so excited that I'd made everyone laugh. Everyone! Even people I'd never spoken to . . . which was most of the class.

It's not like I'd done something really naughty and bad. I'd just told a tiny white lie. Not even a lie, really, because Tab and Tap are so similar-sounding he could easily have misheard me saying Tab. Okay, so my dad's not really a plumber. (If only!) I just thought of saying he was, on the spot. How brilliant was that?!

I'm going to have to think of more funny things to say and do at school so that everyone keeps thinking I'm a laugh. It is *sooooo* cool.

SUMMER TERM WEEK 1

SUNDAY

I **spent the weekend** sorting out my bedroom properly. I've arranged all my stuff from Ivy House, including my favourite chair, which Dad made me before he started drinking so much he wasn't even able to sit on a chair, never mind make one!

It fits perfectly under the desk Gran's put in here so I can, as she sweetly said, 'Do homework in privacy.' Hah, hah. It's not really a desk, it's an old kitchen table, I think. It must be – one of its two drawers had a huge plastic syringe-thingy in it and I think that's for basting a chicken . . . Or else it's for something much more disgusting, which I am not going to think about or even write down, but learnt about in biology and has to do with how lesbian couples have babies. That's completely mank – super mank, actually – so extra mank it's mankenstein!

In fact it must have been a kitchen table, because I've just discovered a packet of biscuits in the drawer – unopened (the biscuits, not the drawer, obvs). The sell-by date was seven months ago but they taste fine. Must try not to eat them all, though. I don't want to be the piggy fat one at school. In fact, I must cut down on snacks. Not like, today, or even tomorrow, but soon . . . perhaps when I've finished these biscuits.

My room's not huge but it's quite nice. It's at the back, overlooking the garden, which is so overgrown and messy you could bury a dead body in there and no one would ever find it. Perhaps that's where Gran's husband is, and not in Canada like everyone thinks.

I've got shelves on either side of a little fireplace for all those books Mum keeps giving me that I don't read, and then my bed is behind the door. That's cool because it means I can see whoever comes in before they see me, so I can pretend to be asleep or dead or whatever, if necessary.

Also, I can stand up on the bed and hide behind the door, if I really squish myself up against the hinges, so when you walk in it looks like my room is empty. I can jump out on top of Luke if he dares to enter my room without permission. That'll so freak him out. He hates being jumped on out of the blue – crybaby.

THIS IS TOP SECRET: I've wedged Muzzy in between my mattress and the wall, so you can't see her if you just walk into my room, unless you know she's there. Which no one is going to, okay? I know I'm a bit grown up to still have the fluffy toy cat I've had since I was a baby, but I can't exactly throw her away, can I? And I don't want to put her in a cupboard as if I don't actually love her. And I do sort of like having her with me at night, sometimes. It's not like I suck my thumb or carry around my blankie with me all the time like that pathetic baby Luke does. And it's good to have someone to talk to when you're on your own.

Anyway, Muzzy's in her special hiding place and I don't have to tell anyone, ever, where she is. I will just know she's right there.

The completely best thing about my room is . . . it's got a lock that works! An actual key that turns in an actual lock that actually works!!! And Gran said, not realising clearly what this meant to me, 'Be careful with that key because it's the only one.' THE ONLY ONE! Mum had a go at Gran when she noticed, and even suggested *she* keep hold of the key, but Gran, of course, just told her not to be silly and said, 'Why would any thirteen-year-old girl even think of locking herself inside her bedroom?' Erm, hello, why wouldn't she, more like?!

Sometimes you'd think Gran hadn't had a daughter of her own. Every teenage girl I've ever met wishes she could lock her bedroom door! I begged Mum and Dad for a lock on my door at Ivy House and they always refused. 'What if there's a fire?' was the best reason they could come up with. Obviously if there'd been a fire I'd have unlocked the door to escape. Duh. I don't think getting a lock on your bedroom door suddenly means you turn into Joan of Arc and so you decide to stay locked in there when your house is burning down.

This is so brilliant – I can have mates round (please, please, let A'isha, Emz and me be best mates, *pleeeeease*) and we can lock ourselves in.

Being able to lock my own bedroom door is so cool. Double cool, in fact, because, I've just checked, Luke's bedroom doesn't have one, and neither does Mum's or Gran's. Actually, the 'special' grown-ups-only loo that only Mum and Gran are supposed to use doesn't even have a lock! Maybe that's why only they are meant to use it, so that we don't walk in on them. Yuck – what a totally mankenstein idea!

It'd be a bit embarrassing having Emz and A'isha round, though. I don't really want them to know that we live with Gran.

BRAINWAVE: what if I pretend Gran is our servant? Or housekeeper? I'd have to ask Gran to go along with it. Would she mind, I wonder?

It's a bit cheeky, but it's not like she'd have to actually *be* a servant, or do anything servanty. She'd just have to pretend to work for us. Though actually she's taken us in because my dad literally spent our house on booze.

Hmm, if people were going to believe she was our servant then she'd have to do something like bring me and my mates tea (if I make any mates) or say something like, 'Shall I run your bath, now?' like servants do on telly. That is so weird – a grown-up running another grown-up's bath.

I suppose you get servants when you're really rich so you don't have to do anything at all, ever. I heard Gran say once that the royal family get their servants to brush their teeth *for* them! Amazeballs! That is *so* extra. As well as super weird and total vom-making-city. Mankenstein.

When she said this, she wasn't talking to me – she was talking to Basil, her dog, while she was brushing *his* teeth. I think she was trying to make him feel better about not being able to brush his own teeth. That's fair enough, cos it's not like any dog can brush its own teeth, but the royal family have hands, which dogs don't. Not even super-spesh Basil, who is, according to Gran, the finest-bred Westie. (And she'd know because she grew him, or whatever doggie-people say, from her last dog who was Basil's mum.) Gran probs wouldn't let him brush his own teeth if he did have hands because she SO loves doing everything for him, just like Mum and Luke. But, pathetic though he is, Luke does at least brush his own teeth.

I know, I know, what is Gran is doing talking to her dog like he's a person, like he's her son? That's because to her he *is* her child!

Gran really does talk to Basil like he's an actual person, you know, with, like, human hearing and who can talk. She jokes that he's only not saying anything back because he's *choosing* not to talk. I don't think she's joking. I don't really mind – I think it's funny – but it drives Mum mad, which is even funnier. Because, obvs, Basil can't actually talk, Gran does this voice for him. So when she thinks he's got something to say *she* says it. It is really bonkers and funny, I have to admit. And *that* drives Mum mad too!

Mum's always going on to Gran that she loves Basil more than her. Gran probably doesn't really but I wouldn't blame her if she did – Mum's much more annoying than Basil, and that includes him not being able to brush his own teeth and barking at the back door when there's no one there.

At least Basil doesn't write a blog. It would be funny if he did – he could call it *Dog Blog!* What would he write about – walks, barks, chasing squirrels, having his teeth brushed by Gran? Hmm, that already sounds more interesting than Mum's boring blog.

By the way, Mum DOES NOT KNOW that I've read her blog. Amazingly it has not occurred to her that of course I would read it! Hellooo? How else am I going to find out what she's saying about me?! Duh.

But it's a secret that no one in the whole entire world knows about except me . . . and Muzzy, obviously.

Of course, apart from moaning about me and her changed life Mum also writes about breaking up with Dad because he's an alcoholic. S'pose she's got a right to do that, but I wish she wouldn't. I don't know, it sort of makes her look a bit losery, too, I think . . . It's not her fault, but choosing him way back makes her a bit to blame, too.

I hate Dad sometimes. He is such a selfish pig. (Oh god, now I sound like Mum!) I wonder how many bottles of wine you get for, say, the price of a school skirt? I might ask him one of these days, super-sarkily, though, obviously . . .

Actually, no point probably, cos, in the end, he won't get what I mean – he never does. Or he'll say something super annoying like 'Darling, how on earth would I know what a school skirt cost?' or 'Are you thinking of trading in your skirt for alcopops,

Tabitha? How naughty!' and then smirk, like he's said something really clever and funny. Why can't he be like other people's dads – just normal and not drunk all the time? I overheard Mum say to Gran the other day, 'If he could hear what anyone was saying to him we wouldn't be here.'

I don't know if she meant 'here', like at Gran's house, in her kitchen (which is where they were) or 'here' in her blog-way, meaning 'in this emotional state'.

Yuk, I hate the way she uses ordinary words that mean something really obvious like 'here' to mean something really not obvious like 'here' as in how she's feeling. She's always talking about the 'bad place' she's in when she's in a really nice room. I just wish she wouldn't say 'bad place' when she means 'unhappy' or 'sad' or something – I wish she'd just use the right words.

SUMMER TERM
WEEK 2
WEDNESDAY

At lunch today (it's been Emz, A'isha and me every day since I met them) A'isha asked if my dad really was a plumber. So I told them about my parents splitting up and my dad staying in the countryside where we used to live. I said my mum and brother and me had moved to London, but I didn't tell them we'd moved in with Gran.

I wasn't exactly lying. I did say Gran lived with us. I just felt funny telling them that we had lived in our own house and now had to live with my mum's mum.

A'isha said her gran lived with them too, so that made me feel a lot better.

I didn't tell them about Greyfriars either. I was worried they'd think I was super posh, which I'm not really, but it's true that schools like that are mainly filled with posh girls. And I didn't tell them about Dad being an alcoholic. I'm not sure I ever will, even if we stay being best friends, which I so hope we will. How do you tell anyone a thing like that? I don't want people to think there's something weird about me, having a dad who's an addict. Most kids' parents are grown-ups with jobs and their own places to live, even if they've split up. *I* don't even understand why Dad is like he is, so I can't really explain it to others, can I?

Emz lives in that road at the top of the hill, not far from Gran's but way nicer, full of detached houses that stand back from the road, and most of them even have gravel driveways! She is really pretty. Not like super make-you-hate-her pretty, just, like, normal she-could-be-my-friend pretty. She's got long brown hair and green eyes and she's quite tall. Well, taller than A'isha and me.

A'isha has huge dark eyes and really long eyelashes, and she always wears mascara so they're, like, super noticeable. I think you notice her eyes more because of her scarf . . . hijab. I must remember to call it that and not scarf. I don't think A'isha would exactly have a major hissy fit if I called it a scarf but I don't want to annoy her. I don't know her well enough yet to risk it. She can call it what she likes but I don't think I can or even should. It's always a bit funny, isn't it, when someone is rude about something that is theirs and then somebody else joins in? You think, 'Hey, I can be as rude as I like about it because it's mine – you can't!' Like, I think – in fact I know – that Luke is a total loser, super-nerd and general waste of oxygen, but even though it's totes what I think about him and is actually factually correct I wouldn't want anyone else saying that about him, obvs.

A'isha is a bit plump, like me. Well, actually, she's a bit thinner than me, but she's not skinny like Emz. I never thought I could like a skinny girl, but Emz isn't skinny in that look-at-me-ooh-I'm-so-thin-I-*never*-eat-biscuits-or-chocolate way, like practically every single girl at Greyfriars was. Honestly, you'd have thought sweet things were made of rat poison the way they all shrieked if I even picked up something fattening.

Gran had sneaked a few chocolate fingers into my lunchbox when Mum wasn't looking this morning. Mum would go mad if she knew. The other day she'd said I should go on a diet. Gran was brilliant. 'Leave her alone, she's a growing girl,' she said. I didn't know the chocolate fingers were in there until we were in the canteen. Emz and A'isha both spotted them first and grabbed one each. Gran had put in three, so there was one for each of us. It was really nice sharing with them.

EAT ME

CHOCOLATE BISCUITS

I walked nearly all the way home with Emz and told her about my super-annoying little brother and how much of a know-it-all he is and how Mum just thinks he's brilliant and everything he does is so much better than anything I do. And then Emz said, 'I'd love a little brother or sister – you *are* lucky'.

I was like, 'Are you serious? Luke's the most annoying

thing in the whole wide world,' but Emz said that it was weird being the only child in a house.

I didn't want to go on and on but she hasn't got a clue how much better life would be without a little gnat always buzzing around me, copying me and touching my things.

When I got back home, Gran was sitting in the kitchen with Basil on her lap, talking to him. 'Well, I never, you do look smart in that hat, Basil, yes you do, very smart indeed. You'll get all the girls wearing that.'

Seriously. My gran was talking to her dog about the thing she had knitted and then put on his head. It was a sort of floppy beret. A mini one, obviously, because a proper-sized one wouldn't fit on a dog's head. It'd be more like a blanket and then the dog wouldn't be able to see. Unless it was an absolutely huge dog, maybe.

'Oh, Tab, darling, did you have a good day? Look, isn't it adorable? I've just finished knitting it.'

I didn't know what to say. Obvs I wanted to ask why Basil – or any dog actually – needed a hat, but I didn't want to be mean so I just sort of shrugged my shoulders and said, 'Yeah.'

'And, best of all, Basil absolutely loves it, don't you,

you clever thing?' Then Gran replied (helloooo?!!!) using her Basil voice, the voice she's decided he talks with (erm, again, helloooo?!!!): 'Yes, Mum, I really like it. It keeps my head warm and cosy and it looks pretty jaunty, too. Thank you for making it for me.'

'You're very welcome, Basil – what lovely manners you have,' Gran replied, in her own voice

I don't know what to do when Gran and Basil have these, erm, conversations. Can you call it a conversation when you're doing both the voices?

When I talk to Muzzy at least I don't reply for her. Because I do *know* she's a toy cat. I actually *know* she doesn't have thoughts or an actual voice. I just like having someone, okay sorry, some kitten, to talk to. And not that much, anyway, now that I'm a teenager. In fact, I'm practically an adult – I can get married in three years' time, after all. Not that I want to, yuck, but, you know, it is a fact and it means I'm three years away from being a grown-up.

I make my gran sound like she is completely round the bend, but she's really not, unless you count talking to a dog, doing a squeaky voice for it and dressing it in clothes she's specially made for it as round the bend.

Actually, I've always thought the voice Gran does for Basil is more appropriate for a mouse than a dog. All that barking would mean Basil always had a sore throat and sore throats make your voice sound gruff, don't they, not squeaky? I prob won't mention that to Gran, though. It's not like it's that important.

Gran asked me to take Basil for a walk. As usual she made me take a poo bag with me – like I'm ever going to use it! (BTW obvs the poo bag is for Basil's poo, not mine, okay?) As soon as I got out of the front door I pulled his beret off and stuffed it into my coat pocket. There was no way I was walking around with a dog wearing a hat, any hat, but especially not a floppy beret. I never wear hats – they make me feel like I'm shouting, 'Hey, everybody look at me, I've got a hat on!'

I decided to walk Basil up towards Emz's road. I don't know the number of her house and obviously

I wasn't going to drop in. What a loser that would make me look! I hope she'll invite me round to hers one day but I was definitely not going to just ring on her doorbell totally randomly, and extra especially not when I've got Basil with me.

But I really wanted to see what the houses up there are like up close. I've only ever seen them from the car – and that was ages ago, before we lived here, when we *had* a car.

It was a bit further away than I'd thought and by the time we got there Basil was pulling on the leash to go back, lazy thing. He just sort of stopped when we got to the top of her road, like he knew he'd done his circuit and that was enough.

We had a tug-of-war. Basil would not budge, no matter how hard I pulled his lead. He dug his claws into a bit of grass next to the pavement. I ended up dragging him along the grass like a sleigh and then finally he gave up and started walking. I don't know what was wrong with him – maybe he was cross I'd taken his hat off.

On the way back home, I spotted this really tall boy. He was walking a dog too, the same type of dog as Basil – a Westie. That's what Gran's told me I must tell people if they ask me what breed he is. Really, though, the only thing that people are going to ask about Basil, if they ask me anything at all, is not what type of dog he is but why is he wearing that silly hat?! Anyway, the boy's dog was really cute and so was he. He was walking in the opposite direction to me, back towards Emz's road. I'll bet he lives there. Lucky him. As we passed each other, even though the pavement was quite wide, our dogs kind of leapt towards each other, both straining at their leads, trying to say 'hello' in that way dogs always do. They were doing it nicely, though, not barking and yapping.

The boy and I both sort of stopped and tried to drag our dogs away, but without looking at each other, only at our dogs. Well, I was looking at him a bit, obvs, otherwise I wouldn't have known he wasn't looking at me.

I think he's a year or so older than me and has lovely, glossy dark brown hair, a bit long, just to his shoulders, and dark brown eyes, like swirls of melted chocolate. He was so gorgeous. I didn't want to smile at him or say hello or do anything that would make me look silly or uncool. But just as we were about to turn away from each other he smiled at me, in a really friendly way, and looked at Basil and then his dog and said 'Snap.' Because we both had the same type of dog. How hilarious is that?

Oh my god, just as that dishy boy was walking away, and I mean right at that absolute second, Basil decided to do a poo. I could have killed him. I was so nervous the boy was going to turn around and see my dog having a stinky poo on the pavement. It was almost as if Basil was pooing *at* him! I knew I had to pick it up. I really wanted to just leave it there, but I knew the boy might see if I left it so I couldn't. It was so mankenstein – Basil's poo was still warm, I could feel it through the plastic. Talk about vom-making-city. Mind you, I'll bet that boy picks up his dog's poo, so that makes it a bit better.

I really hope I see him again. I'm going to offer to take Basil out every day. I must think of something funny to say next time I see him. Thank god I'd taken Basil's hat off! He would've thought I was totally mad if he'd seen me walking a dog wearing that.

SUMMER TERM
WEEK 2

THURSDAY

Yuck, Luke is disgusting. Completely and totally repulsive, sick-making, vomit-inducing, mank-of-mankenstein revolting. Even though I've told him a gazillion times he must never, ever use the loo in the bathroom and only use the one downstairs, he still uses the one in the bathroom!!! I could kill him.

'It's not your personal, private bathroom,' he whined, 'and anyway it's two floors down to the other loo from my room and it's dark and freezing there.' Pathetic baby – it's because he's frightened of the dark.

I know it's not actually *my* bathroom (so wish it

was) but he shouldn't use it unless he's going to treat it exactly the way I do. He always leaves the loo seat up and it's *soooo* annoying. This morning it was up – he must have gone to the loo in the night – so I sat down without looking and sat straight on the china bit. Eeeurgh! It's all Luke's fault because he's the only boy in the house and no one else puts the seat up, obviously. And Gran and Mum never use it because of having their own special no-lock-on-the-door bathroom.

I had a brilliant idea. I got one of those Post-it notes Gran uses to leave instructions all around the house about how to open this or that door, or what day the bins go out, or what not to touch in the fridge. I got a really brightly coloured, huge one and wrote on it, in massive capital letters:

PLEASE AIM YOUR URINE PRECISELY
TO BE SURE IT DOES NOT GO ON THE
SEAT AND ONLY INTO THE WATER
INSIDE THE LOO.

And then, just to be super sarcastic, underneath I put:

THANK YOU FOR YOUR CO-OPERATION.
(PS USE THE DOWNSTAIRS LOO!)

And then I put the note up on the wall above the loo in my, okay, *the* bathroom. Luke is going to be so embarrassed when he sees that because he'll know it's for him. I would hardly be writing a note to Gran or Mum about aiming their pee, would I?

When I left for school Mum was in the kitchen, drinking a cup of coffee and already on her computer. Way back, before she got married (or 'Parked my brain', as she says) she was a journalist, apparently, and now she's reckons she's writing articles again, but I don't know who she thinks they're for! I bet she was actually writing her blog – though what could she have to say that's happened between last night, when she was last on it (for the whole evening, practically), and this morning? *Woke up, walked downstairs, made myself*

coffee, annoyed my daughter as per usual? Soooo interesting.

Anyway Mum, whose hair is quite long (too long, I think, for an old woman) had swooped her hair up, all messily, into a sort of bun and stuck a pencil in it to keep it up. She's done it loads of times and I never thought anything about it. But today it gave me a brilliant idea for what to do at school. Since making the whole class laugh with the my-plumber-dad-called-me-Tap thing, I've been trying to come up with more things to do that'll make everyone laugh.

I want them all to know it wasn't just a one-off. I loved it when everyone laughed because I'd got the better of the teacher. It's definitely true that he just hadn't known what to say. I don't want to be mean. I don't hate teachers. I'm not a proper horrible person. But I do want to stand out. I want to be noticed. I really want to be popular and the only way I can think of to be popular is to be the one at school who'll say and do things no other kid would dare to say or do. It's not like if I get A*s in everything and behave really well and do everything I'm told to do. I'm going to become cool. No one ever got cool that way and no one ever thinks those kinds of kids are cool. Just look at Grace.

Grace actually put her hand up when a teacher asked if anyone wanted to volunteer to be a playground litter picker-upper! Yuckarama, that is so mankenstein! She was the only one, of course. I can't believe anyone would agree to do that. The school does give you extra merit points for doing it but still, it's not worth it for how nerdy you're going to look picking up rubbish with one of those sticks with a claw at the end. Oh man, there is no way I'd do that. That is so extra. Grace is always so extra, I've decided.

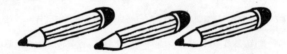

Anyway, I decided to put my genius pencil-plan to use during Ms Cameron's class. I chose her class because she always flies off the handle at the smallest thing, even something tiny like someone asking if they can be excused to go to the toilet!

I didn't tell Emz and A'isha I was going to do it, either. I decided it would be best if I just did it and then acted all normal and like, 'What?'

Just before the class started I got three pencils, twizzled my hair round and round really tightly and then put it up into a bun, like Mum's was this morning but much neater and tighter, and I stuck the pencils in at different angles and across each other to hold the hair in place. It looked almost like a fashion thing, like it was meant and could (almost) be an actual hair accessory you buy, which is exactly what I'd planned.

When we went into class, a few people were giving me, or rather my hair, weird looks, but I just ignored them. Without looking up from her desk, Ms Cameron told us all to pick up the prepared sheet that she'd put out and to start filling in the answers.

Oh no, she had to see my hair or my plan wasn't going to work. I didn't know what to do. At our table, Emz said, 'What have you done with your hair?' and then A'isha said, 'You look like a Japanese woman. Miss is going to go mad.'

'That's the plan,' I replied and we all started giggling.

Ms Cameron looked up. 'Who's making that noise?' she barked at last.

'Sorry, Miss,' Emz said, and immediately started doing the work and so did A'isha.

And then Ms Cameron saw me, looked at my hair and asked, really snippily, 'Tabitha Baird, what on earth have you done with your hair?'

Everyone stopped what they were doing and looked at me, waiting for what I was going to say. This is exactly what I'd hoped. It was brilliant knowing everyone was watching.

'My hair, Miss? I don't know what you mean.' I stayed completely straight-faced, like I had no idea what she was talking about.

'Your hair. You seem to have a number of pencils in your hair. It looks ridiculous. Those pencils should be stored in your pencil case, not in your hair,' she continued, obviously quite pleased with her little joke about the correct place for storing pencils.

'Ah, I see. Oh no, Miss, these aren't *those* kind of pencils. These are pencils specifically for holding up your hair – it's the latest fashion.'

I could hear a few people start to laugh.

'Don't be silly. Take them out now.'

'But I can't, Miss, they're holding my hairdo – my

bun – up. It took me all morning to do this before I came to school.'

Ms Cameron looked at me for a minute, obviously trying to decide what to do. I could feel the whole class waiting for what was going to happen next. I didn't flinch. I just stared back at her doing my absolute best I-don't-understand-what-the-problem-is face.

Miss was obviously expecting me to crumble before she did and when I didn't I could tell she was getting crosser and crosser. You could hear a pin drop.

Eventually she practically barked, 'Tabitha, take those pencils out of your hair immediately!'

I waited a minute and then said, 'Miss, I'm not being rude, but maybe you aren't completely up on modern fashion. I've seen this bun done on telly and everything.'

The whole class burst out laughing. Ms Cameron looked like she was going to explode. I just stared back at her, all nicely. I even managed to look around at the others who were laughing and do a what-are-you-all-laughing-about? face.

'I will not put up with this cheek, Tabitha. Leave my class this minute,' Miss eventually managed to splutter.

As I stood up I said, 'Okay, if you're sure, but, you know, it's just a teen fashion look – it's all the rage,' and the whole class laughed again.

I had to wait outside until the lesson was over and that was a bit boring. But when everyone came out, oh man, everyone, including people I'd never really spoken to before, said things like, 'That was so funny,' and, 'Oooh, you really got Miss there,' and one boy even high-fived me.

Emz and A'isha came out of the class last. 'Tab, you are so brave. That was so daring. How did you manage not to crack up?' A'isha said.

It felt so good to have them say those things. I think I have definitely found the way to be cool and I'm loving it. Ms Cameron gave me a half-hour detention after school tomorrow, though, which is super boring, but worth it because the hair thing was so great.

I **got home** and asked Gran if she wanted me to take Basil out for a walk. Mum nearly splurted coffee out of her mouth all over her computer on the kitchen table. I tried to take the mick by sarcastically imitating Mum's splurting, but nearly choked on the apple I was eating instead. (I'm trying not to eat biscuits and stuff like that when I get back from school. It is *soooo* hard.)

'Where's my usual daughter gone?!' she cried. Hah, hah, very funny. 'Are you an alien? Have you abducted my permanently stroppy daughter and replaced her with this nice, helpful one?' Mum went on, talking very slowly, pretending she had to speak like that so that the alien – i.e. me – would understand her.

'Mum, stop being so incredibly annoying!' I shouted at her. (She deserved it.) 'I am being nice to Gran. Can't you just leave it? Can't I be nice to Gran and take Basil for a walk without you being so stupid and sarcastic?'

Gran laughed and Mum hissed, 'Not helpful,' under her breath, but I heard. I love it when Gran annoys Mum, because then Mum gets a taste of her own medicine.

Gran just ignored Mum and started talking to Basil, telling him what a lucky boy he was to go out walking with me.

As usual Mum, who literally, physically cannot *not* have a go at me whenever she gets a chance, said, 'I'm just very surprised at Tabitha's sudden willingness to take you out, Basil. Last time she said she'd rather – what was it? – oh yes, have boiling hot oil poured into her ears than take you for a walk. I wonder if there's another dog you like, or perhaps Tabitha likes another dog's walker . . . Has my darling little pudding made a little friend?!'

'Shut up, Mum. This is not funny!' I shouted back.

Mum just said, 'Oh no, darling, I was talking to Basil, not you.'

But I knew she was talking to me and just pretending to be talking to Basil to make me even more annoyed.

Gran then butted in, 'Kat, don't talk to Basil. You know he doesn't understand you, do you, Basil? You only understand your mummy, isn't that right, my own little lad?'

And, at last, that got Mum annoyed. She hates it when Gran talks to Basil like he's her actual child and like she loves him more than her – it's hilarious.

Gran obviously wanted to wind Mum up because she said to Basil, as she was putting yet another ridiculous hat on him (this one was a sort of baby's bonnet – like that was going to stay on once I'd left!), 'Ooh, Basil, your sister is jealous of you.'

Then Mum screamed, 'Mum, stop it. He is a dog, he is not a human being, he is *not* my brother!' and then Basil started barking (but I think that was really because I was jangling his lead underneath the flap of my coat so that Mum couldn't see.)

Gran said, 'Stop it now, Kat. Grow up, you're upsetting Basil!'

Mum gritted her teeth and growled at Basil and then stormed out of the room. It was so funny. Mum is such a baby around Basil. She is properly jealous of him.

Gran brought Basil over to me and clipped his lead on. 'Honestly, my two, they're like cat and dog, the way they fight.'

That's Gran's favourite joke, because Mum is called Kat, short for Katherine. So she says 'cat' but means 'Kat'. She probably only called Mum Katherine so she could shorten it to Kat because when someone says 'cat' you always immediately think of dogs, don't you? Gran's always had dogs and Mum reckons Gran has always preferred every single dog she's had to her.

I don't think that can be actually true. Although it is true that Gran definitely *pretends* to love Basil more than Mum. I feel a bit sorry for Mum. Yuck. I don't like feeling sorry for Mum – must stop that. Must remember at all times that Mum is THE most annoying person in the entire universe – apart from Luke, who shares joint first prize with Mum.

Therefore I don't ever, ever have to feel sorry for either of them because they are the TOP most annoying people in the world.

So I took Basil out and, yes, maybe I was hoping to see Snap-Dog Boy, but I was also trying to be nice to Gran, okay? But that does not mean Mum was right. I went the same way as last time, up round near Emz's road, and I didn't see Snap-Dog Boy at all. Then, just as I was heading home and, I admit, feeling a little disappointed, I spotted him on the other side of the road.

He was running with his dog so I realised there was going to be no chance of organising an accidental bumping-into-him again.

I didn't know what to do. I didn't want to miss this chance. And then, almost without knowing I was going to do it, I called out, 'Hello, Snap-Dog!'

To make matters worse, I don't think he heard me the first time, so rather than be relieved he hadn't heard me, for some reason I shouted it again but louder.

That time he stopped and looked over but obviously didn't know who I was. Oh man, I thought I'd die of embarrassment. What an idiot! He'd stopped and was now looking at me, so I couldn't just walk away and pretend I'd never called anything out, which I obviously now wished I hadn't!

I had to do something, so I pointed at his dog and then mine and called out (again!), 'You said "snap" the other day. Hah, hah! Same dogs, snap!'

I felt like such a complete moron. I mean, what kind of nutter calls out to someone who is running and who they've never even spoken to properly in the first place? He must think I am THE most pathetic person in the entire world. He must think I'm so desperate for friends I have to call out to people who are miles away and running, just to make lame conversation about having similar dogs.

He sort of smiled and shouted back, 'Oh yeah,' and then, 'Okay, see you around, I've got to keep running,' and sped off down the road.

I wished I hadn't called out at all but seeing as I

did it was really good that he said, 'See you around,' wasn't it? Obviously he's expecting (hoping, maybe?) to see me around. That's good, isn't it? That's the sort of thing you say to people you know you'll see around, don't you? So that means he's thought about it, about seeing me around. I mean, if he hadn't ever thought about seeing me again he wouldn't have said that, would he?

When I got home I went on Facebook to see if I could find Snap-Dog Boy, even though Mum would go mad if she knew I was on it. She says it's where creepy, weird men try to find young girls. She knows nothing about the privacy settings and how people actually get access to your page or anything, and there's no point in trying to explain it to her – she just would not get it. Grown-ups just go on and on about being aware of 'online vulnerability' and 'internet risk', which is hilarious as no grown-up knows how to use the internet as well as me and my friends do.

Actually Luke knows his way around a computer and the internet better than anyone. I guess he would though, because being such a nerdy geek he spends most of his life on one.

It turned out to be quite hard to find someone when you don't know their name — surprise, surprise, he doesn't call himself Snap-Dog Boy on Facebook. That's if he is even on there. He must be. Everyone is.

In fact, there is no one called Snap-Dog Boy on Facebook anywhere in the world — there are loads and loads called Dog Boy, but who cares about them? I am only interested in finding Snap-Dog Boy!

SUMMER TERM WEEK 3

WEDNESDAY

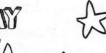

OH MY GOD IN WAY UP HIGH HEAVEN! You would not believe what happened today.

I got into school, as per normal day, i.e. super-boring, boring lessons, boring teachers, you know, regular, boring normal day.

Then at break A'isha got a magazine out of her bag. She'd bought it because it had someone – can't remember who – she liked on the cover. So, Emz and me were chatting away and then A'isha threw a plastic, see-through pouch sort of thing with a load of coloured rings inside it at us. 'Here, do you want these? They came free with this mag.'

Emz and I opened the bag. There were about six rings — they were all different, really bright, neony colours and quite nice and cool. So, as a joke, I put them all on one finger, sort of stacked up on top of each other. They were tight in the first place and the more rings I put on, the harder I had to push to get them on because, obviously, there wasn't really enough room on my finger for all of them. After I'd got all six of them on, I waved my be-ringed hand about a bit, like I was flashing diamonds, and everyone laughed.

Then I realised that I couldn't bend my knuckle. It started to get a bit uncomfortable so I tried to take them off and I couldn't! I was pulling and pulling and they just would not budge.

And then my finger started swelling up in the spaces in between the rings and went all puffy and looked like a big, fat uncooked sausage. And then it started to hurt and the squished sausagey bit started to throb.

A'isha just kept laughing her head off. 'Look at the colour your finger's gone. That is gross,' she said, super helpfully, between chokes of laughter. It did look pretty mankenstein.

Anyway, it was hurting so much and I just could not get the rings to move, so Emz suggested we went to the toilets and all tried to pull them off using water and soap, but that didn't work either.

And then Emz, who's always the most sensible out of us three I have to admit, freaked out. 'Oh my god, what if the rings have cut your finger's blood supply off?' she said. 'We'll have to go to medical before your finger drops off.'

I was beginning to worry that it actually might. It had gone a sort of deep purple and had stopped throbbing. I couldn't feel it at all by this time.

In medical, the useless pretend-nurse who, A'isha says, always tells you to lie down no matter what you go in there for — stomach-ache, headache, football injury — didn't actually tell me to lie down. Instead she looked really worried. 'Oh dear, that does look awful,' she said helpfully. 'Why did you put all those rings on?'

'Because I thought it might be a great way of getting my finger to drop off cos I don't really need that one,' I replied, a bit super-sarcastically because I thought that was a really stupid question. At least A'isha snorted with laughter, but Emz gave me a come-on-this-is-serious look.

The nurse took the hand with the bad finger, pushed it a bit, ignoring my cries of pain, sucked air in between her pursed lips, shook her head and then said, 'Right, we've got to get you to a hospital. These rings must come off as soon as possible.'

I was a bit freaked-out and like, 'Hospital? Isn't that a bit heavy? Can't we just sort of, I don't know, stamp on the rings to break them?'

Emz, being sensible again, pointed out that, as the rings were actually on my finger, if we stamped on them, that would mean stamping on my finger, which might break at the same time as the rings.

She had a point. So the nurse called the school office to get someone to come and take me to hospital and told A'isha and Emz to go back to class. It was all a bit serious by then and didn't seem so much fun without my pals.

This 'behaviour monitor', Ms Cantor, turned up to take me to the hospital. She was a really young woman, not that much older than me, and looked nice and friendly.

The hospital's nearby, but Miss drove me there in her car because she said she thought it was getting urgent.

While we were waiting at A&E, Ms Cantor, who said I should call her by her first name, Eva – cool, eh? – told me that her job at the school was trying to keep bad behaviour 'in check'. She wants to be a teacher but needs to experience a school before starting her training.

'So, basically,' I said, 'you're there as a sort of unofficial police officer, but with no real powers, to keep an eye on the out-of-control kids.' I meant to be cheeky but I was also telling the truth because that is what she's there for, isn't it? All the bad kids know members of staff don't have that much power – except, I suppose, they can get them expelled, but it takes a lot for that to happen.

She actually laughed when I said that though, which made me like her more. It was quite easy talking to her so I didn't think she'd go mad when I said I thought teaching would be the worst job in the whole wide world.

'Helping shape a young mind, especially a quick one like yours, is probably one of the most important and rewarding jobs in the world,' she replied calmly.

No one has ever said I've got a quick mind before. Actually I don't think anyone's ever said anything at all about my mind before. A couple of teachers back at Greyfriars told me 'You're not fulfilling your potential' but there they probably meant my potential to own a pony and get my hair dyed blonde.

I didn't let on, but I was actually quite pleased. It's not like saying I'm a swot – it's just like saying I'm bright, which I am, I hope. I just don't want to do any schoolwork. Who does?

Anyway, we got shown into a cubicle and a young, quite good-looking male doctor, Dr Tarbath, came along and checked my finger out. While he was examining it I gave Miss a he's-not-bad look and she smirked back at me and we both laughed. It was weird behaving with a sort-of teacher like I'd normally behave with my mates.

'Right, I've had a look and there's nothing else for it, I'm afraid – this finger is going to have to come off,' the doctor said.

Miss gasped out loud. I felt sick and wanted to cry. Oh god, my whole life was going to be over with only four fingers on one hand – how completely and totally mankenstein would that be?

'What?! You aren't serious, are you?' Miss asked him.

'Please tell me you're not serious,' I said, really trying hard not to cry.

The doctor looked at Eva like, 'I'm very sorry but it can't be helped,' and gave me a long, sympathetic look.

Then he started laughing and said, 'Of course I'm not. I'm pulling your leg. Or rather your finger.'

And before I knew it, he'd got out a large pair of blunt, scissory things, and started cutting off each plastic ring. 'That's the end of your precious rings, though, I'm sorry to tell you,' he said, as he clipped off the last one.

'Thank you so much, doctor,' Eva said to him as

I was massaging my finger back to life. It had lost all feeling, like super-bad cramp.

The doctor smiled back at her. I think they both liked each other. 'Are you going back to school?' he asked, and when Miss said we were, he turned to me. I thought he was going to give a big, long lecture about being stupid for jamming so many rings onto my finger and wasting doctor's time and all that sort of boring grown-up stuff, but what he actually said was, 'Shall we play a little trick on your schoolmates?' I couldn't believe a doctor could be so cool.

He took some bandages and strapped the finger that the rings had been on to the palm of my hand from the knuckle down so it looked like the top was cut off. Then he wound more bandages around the whole hand leaving the other three fingers free from the knuckles up.

'Right, that'll do it. Tell them I had to amputate your finger to get the rings off!'

When I held up my hand, it really did look like my finger had been cut off.

MISSING
FINGER!!!

When we drove back, Miss told me she'd got the doctor's number. So cool, and all thanks to my finger! By the time we got back it was second break and Miss left me at the door of the canteen and gave me a big wink. I went in, making sure I had a really sad, boo-hoo-poor-me face on.

Emz and A'isha rushed straight up to me. I didn't say anything (I knew I couldn't or I'd have laughed out loud). I just held up my hand.

They both literally shrieked out loud at the sight of my hand with the 'missing' finger, and everyone in the canteen looked over at us. A few people came over to see what was going on, including Grace. I explained that my finger had had to be amputated because of 'the onset of gangrene' (that's what the doctor told me to say).

Everyone was a bit shocked and then, guess what? Grace fainted! She actually fainted. How extra is that? I saw her look at my hand and then at me, and then she swooned and dropped dead, right onto the floor! Everyone suddenly crowded round her to see if she was all right.

I was a bit annoyed because I was the one with a

real, well, okay, not *actually* real, but they thought it was a real, genuine amputation. I had actually 'lost a finger' but now they were more worried about someone who'd just fainted!

Luckily Grace came to pretty quickly and everyone went back to asking me what had happened, what the doctors had said and where the cut-off finger was. I hadn't thought about that, but I said the hospital had kept it. I wanted to say it was in my bag. It would have been awesome to see people's faces when I told them that – Grace would have fainted again, for sure!

It was so brilliant! Absolutely no one realised it was a joke. Not one single person asked me if it was really true. I could not believe it.

I felt bad about not telling Emz and A'isha the truth. When it was going-home time and we were walking along, loads of other kids gave me pitying looks and nudged each other and pointed at me. Emz and A'isha put themselves either side of me, sort of like protection, so then I decided to tell them. I had to. I couldn't keep it a secret any longer.

They both doubled over, holding their sides laughing. I was so pleased, and relieved, because I was worried one of them, most likely Emz, would be cross that I hadn't told them straightaway.

When I got home, I tried pretending to Mum that I had had my finger cut off, but before I even got to the actual true stuff about going to hospital and everything, Luke said, 'I can see the top of your so-called amputated finger bulging underneath all that stupid bandaging.' I could have killed him.

Mum said, 'Oh darling, you are so clever, only ten years old and you know the word amputated.'

Luke replied, 'Of course I do and I can spell it, too.'

So, no one was paying the slightest bit of attention to me or my story. As per usual. I almost wished I had actually had my finger cut off and then they'd have been sorry, huh?

Later on, I Instagrammed a picture of my hand showing all my fingers on it. I didn't want everyone to think that I really had lost a finger forever. That would be mankenstein and not funny.

SUMMER TERM
WEEK 3

THURSDAY

As I **walked** into school today I noticed various groups of kids from various different years giving me looks that were a mixture of yuck-did-she-really-lose-a-finger? to wow-she's-at-school-the-day-after-losing-her-finger, and then smiles from the ones who'd obviously seen it on Instagram, like they thought it was funny and a brilliant prank. It felt really good to know that so many people had heard about my stupendous joke.

As I made my way to the classroom I super casually waggled my left hand around to show it had ALL of my fingers on it. I didn't bother to check people's reactions. I felt a thousand metres tall. I could not believe I'd done something that so many others had heard about. It was just totally, completely brilliant – the best feeling in the world. The amputated finger had made me a legend. It felt like it didn't matter any more that I wasn't the prettiest or thinnest girl – it felt like I had earned a new status because I was the most daring, the bravest, possibly even the funniest girl at school. I had managed to convince an entire school that I had had a whole finger cut off and during school time, too! It was amazing.

MISSING FINGER!!!

But, just as I got to class a Year 7 kid, who I'd never seen before, came up to me. 'Are you the girl who pretended to have her finger cut off?' he panted, all out of breath. I was just about to explain my brilliant wheeze when he went on, 'The head, Miss Wright, wants to see you in her office now,' and then he shot off.

'Oh great,' I thought. 'I'll bet she isn't going to

think my fake amputation is as hilarious as everyone else obviously does.'

And I was soooo right. Hah, hah! I was right about Miss Wright. Geddit?

I went down and knocked on the door of her office. Mrs Brassington, the secretary (who, Emz had told me, everyone calls Mrs Bras because she's got the most enormous boobs – she so does!), nodded at me through the glass panel to come in.

'Hmm,' was all she said, in a really grumpy way, when I entered. Obviously she'd heard what I'd done and her grumpy 'hmm' was her letting me know what she thought. Like, I could care less what Mrs Bras thinks of me. Actually she should really be called Mrs No-Bra-Fits-Me because her boobs seemed to spill out of every side of her bra – her top half was like a mountain range of squishy lumps and bumps.

'Send her in!' I heard Miss Wright call out from her lair – the inner office where she lurks.

Mrs Bras raised her eyebrows at me, really high, like she was saying, 'You're in for it now.'

I scowled back at her and walked into the head's office.

'Tabitha Baird, it has come to my attention that following an incident involving some plastic rings you pretended to have a finger amputated,' Miss Wright said, without even asking me to sit down!

'Yeah . . . and?' I replied, deciding I might as well go for it. Well, there was no point in pretending I hadn't done it and I wasn't about to apologise . . . not straight away, that was for sure.

'You have caused a number of people a considerable amount of distress. People who genuinely believed you had a major disfiguration, an *amputation* . . .'

I had to stop myself laughing at that point.

'. . . I gather one pupil, Grace McKnight, even fainted.'

Oh god, I just knew it'd somehow be my fault pathetic Grace had fainted! I didn't make her faint. I didn't even wave my 'missing' finger in her face. I can't help it if she's that wet. It is not my fault.

I didn't say anything back though. I knew she was waiting for me to apologise, but I was not going to.

'Have you got anything to say for yourself, Tabitha?' Miss Wright eventually said after we'd both left a long gap, each of us waiting for the other to speak first.

And it was her! Miss Wright spoke first! Result.

I hate it when grown-ups ask that. They definitely do not expect you to say what you've *really* got to say for yourself, like, 'Yeah, I thought it was hilarious and so did everyone else and I'm definitely going to do something like that again,' that is for sure. So, they don't really mean, 'Have you got anything to say for yourself?' They actually mean, 'Are you going to say what *I* want you to say?'

'Erm, not really, I just did it for a laugh,' I replied, super casually, which was like a way-politer version of what I wanted to say.

I thought about saying it was the doctor's idea in the first place, but I didn't want to drop him in it, especially if he was going to go out with Miss Cantor, and also it kind of made the whole thing seem less brilliant if I admitted it hadn't actually been my very own idea.

'I take a dim view of this whole episode, Tabitha. It can hardly be said you've made a good impression since your arrival. As a consequence you are now "on notice". I will be watching your behaviour with a keen eye,' Miss Wright said, using the tone of voice that means, 'Do not reply, you have been warned, now leave.'

I suppose I should have felt worried and upset, but I didn't, I felt the exact opposite. I felt brilliant! I was really beginning to make my mark here at HAC. Miss Wright was *soooooo* wrong – I actually *had* made 'a good impression' since my arrival, obvs just not in the way Miss Wright meant, but in the way that mattered to me. I *so* had! I mean, if I'd done something bad enough to get called into the head's office then that officially meant I was pretty cool. Also, I don't happen to believe my finger-joke thing was that bad anyway. I'm sure Grace fainting had made it seem like a much bigger deal than it really was but, I have to admit, I was glad it had got me into the head's office.

After class I went up to Grace and said, 'Thanks a lot for telling the head I made you faint.' Although I didn't really mind, I felt like I had to let her know that I knew she'd snitched on me.

'I didn't tell her – someone else must have,' Grace

replied softly, almost whispering. I felt a bit bad because she was obviously telling the truth, but she is quite annoying with the whole shy, nerdy don't-look-at-me thing she has going on, plus the oh-so-extra hairband thing, you know?

At lunch Emz and A'isha were full of questions about what had happened with Miss Wright. Emz said, 'It's quite bad if you have to go to the head's office, you know, Tab?'

'Yeah, you don't want to get suspended or anything, do you?' A'isha chipped in.

'I am so not going to get suspended, trust me. It was just a lark. You don't get suspended for playing a prank.'

And that is true – no one gets kicked out of a school for that sort of thing. But I could tell both of them were a bit worried that I might end up getting into real trouble and that made me feel so good – they cared about what happened to me.

I hadn't wanted Mum and Dad to break up and I hadn't wanted to have to live at Gran's, but because of that, I've now got something I've never really had before — two really good mates who seem to like me as much I like them. And that is the best thing in the whole entire world.

Later on, during study period (where you're supposed to study quietly, obvs, but everyone just talks and then if a teacher shushes us we pretend we were talking about the thing we're studying . . . and the teachers believe us!), I told Emz and A'isha about Snap-Dog Boy.

They couldn't stop laughing at the name I'd given him! A'isha suggested I talk properly to him next time I see him instead of calling out across a busy road to get his attention.

'Duh, like I hadn't thought of that,' I replied, sarkily. 'But what do I say? "Oh hello, we've got the same dog, how funny, but then you'd already noticed that and said 'snap' when I saw you, so, like, you already know we've got the same dog." Hmm, that's going to make me look really cool and brilliant.'

'You don't have to say anything about dogs. Ask him if he lives near, or where he goes to school. You know, a normal, non-dog-related question,' A'isha said.

We started laughing because we all realised that a non-dog-related question would be basically any question in the world anyone could ever think of asking, because most questions are non-dog-related. Unless you work in a kennel, I s'pose.

DOG QUESTIONS

When I got home, guess what? Mum was on her computer, almost certainly writing her blog. What a surprise. Honestly, I think she's addicted to it – addicted to moaning about her life, which is basically what her blog is. She is literally never off it.

'What exactly is so fascinating about your blog, Mum?' I asked, partly because I wanted to annoy her, but also because I didn't want her to notice I was getting biscuits out of the cupboard where Gran's told me she hides them – not from me, obvs, she's all right about me eating biscuits, but from Mum who would take them, not to eat them herself but to stop me finding them.

'I've created a wonderful support network for single mums like me, darling, and I am not blind, please don't eat biscuits, my fat little sausage. They aren't good for you, and you can't afford to eat things like that, which are filled with sugar,' she said without even looking up from her keyboard.

I hate the way Mum goes on about what I eat as if I was some sort of 'special case' – a huge lump who will eat everything in sight if not monitored night and day by a control freak – her!

I didn't reply, but as I put the biscuits away I stuffed another two into my mouth. I didn't even want them. I'd only wanted two or so in the first place, but I ate the extra ones just to annoy Mum and let her know that she can't control what I eat.

And then I realised that as Mum hadn't actually seen me eat the two extra biscuits then there's no way it could really annoy her – and *then* I realised that if I put on weight because of eating extra biscuits, that *will* annoy her. She always mentions it immediately if she thinks I'm looking fatter. How's this, though – Luke gets uglier and spottier every day and she never says anything to him about that!

I don't want to get fatter, obviously – even to annoy Mum. And I am not trying to get fatter, but I should be able to eat a biscuit now and again without my own personal police-officer mother going on and on about how bad biscuits are for me and how fat I'm going to get.

I'm upset now. The only thing Mum ever seems to notice about me is how fat or thin I am. She never asks me about school or homework (which is just as well, I guess, since I don't do homework very often!) or if I'm missing Dad or anything. Come to think of it, Mum only mentions Dad when she's complaining about him and blaming him for losing everything, and why we've had to come and live here.

Gran's the one who asks all those normal mum-type questions, which is one of the really nice things about living here. Luckily Gran's a bit too scatty and her memory's not great, so when she asks about homework I usually say I haven't got any or I've done it or whatever and she never checks up. Result.

SUMMER TERM WEEK 4

TUESDAY

Usually I love getting what Ms Osborne insists on calling 'negative attention', i.e. when the teachers keep having to tell me off for whatever funny thing I'm doing in class and everyone is laughing and egging me on — except, of course, the teacher! I definitely want everyone to think I'm cool at HAC and it looks like that is working out.

But there is such a thing as justice. It's not like I'm naughty and rude *all* the time, so I don't deserve to get into trouble for something I haven't even actually done. But get this . . .

Today we had a supply teacher for lesson three.

She walked into class and, before doing anything else including putting her books down, she said, 'Which one of you is Tabitha Baird?'

Obviously everyone looked at me, so I made a face and, after what I'd decided was a long enough pause to annoy her, but not send her over the edge, said 'Me', but not very loudly, so that she'd have to look around the classroom and sort of guess where the 'me' came from.

But she didn't, she looked straight at me, like she'd known all along it was me – and also everyone was looking at me, so, like, duh – and said, 'Right, I've heard all about you, Tabitha Baird, and I'm not going to wait for you to disrupt this class as, I'm told, you inevitably will.' She then looked quickly around the room and spotted an empty table at the front. (Of course it was empty. No one ever chooses to sit up front, not even Grace.) 'Please sit there where I can keep an eye on you and you won't be able to disturb anyone.'

I was stunned. I could not believe it. I happened not to have even been talking when she'd walked into the room.

I was not about to take this lying down. I wouldn't

have minded so much if I had actually done something, but I hadn't . . . Well, not by then, obviously – I hadn't had a chance. And it doesn't matter if I had been going to do something to wind her up. The fact is, I was completely innocent and she was judging me without a fair trial. I was really cross.

'If you don't mind me saying, Miss, I don't think that's very fair. I might have been misrepresented by the staff you heard talking about me or I might have turned over a new leaf since then,' I said to her.

A few of the class sniggered, which I was pleased about, but them doing that obviously wasn't going to help make Miss believe what I was saying.

'Very funny, now pick up your things and come over here, right now,' she said.

I looked at Emz and A'isha, and gave them a really sad look. I wasn't joking, I *was* sad.

A'isha laughed – typical. I think she thought I was putting it on. But Emz gave me a sad look back. I really, really didn't want to sit away from them and I really, really didn't want to sit on my own. On my own! I mean, what is the point of being at school in the first place, if you can't sit with your best friends and chat?

I would literally, actually, in real life, die of boredom if I just sat in class and only did the boring work the stupid teachers give us. I don't know how anyone just does that.

I picked my things up as noisily as I could, stomped over to the table she'd pointed at, and then dragged the chair out really slowly so it scraped on the floor loudly.

Miss didn't bat an eyelid though. Oh man, she's a tough one.

When the bell went, I gave Miss a super-growly stare but she just said, 'Goodbye, Tabitha, I hope you saw the benefits of working on your own.'

What a smarty-pants. If we have her again I am definitely, definitely going to have to get the better of her.

At lunch Emz asked A'isha and me if we wanted to go round to hers after school on Friday! How cool is that? I'm so pleased. I can't wait to see what her parents are like. If they're rich their house is going to be huge and they'll probably be lovely. Rich people usually have no problems and so are much calmer and nicer than people like Mum.

Mum was calmer before Dad lost everything. Not that we were ever rich, but we were richer than we are now which is can't-even-afford-school-lunches poor.

A'isha's on free school meals, so I guess her family must be quite poor too. I wonder if we're poor enough for free school meals. I don't think Mum knows about them. Hmm, can't decide whether to tell her or not. I think I'd feel a bit funny about being on free school meals, even though A'isha is. I don't know why – maybe it's because it means you are definitely, *officially* poor.

There are loads of kids on free school meals at HAC and it's not like they're any different to the rest of us, or anyone even knows or cares. Maybe I'm just getting used to my new life. I don't know, it still feels a bit weird, but I do like Emz and A'isha *waaaay* more than anyone at my old school.

When I got home Luke and Mum were playing Scrabble at the kitchen table. Please shoot me now. Scrabble? What kind of kid actually wants to play Scrabble, and worst of all with their own mother? I know the answer to that already – my little brother Luke. Luke is that kind of kid. A swotty, goody-two-shoes, nerdy suck-up with no friends. If he'd been playing with Gran then I'd have thought okay, cos it is a sort of granny's game, isn't it, and it's nice to do things for Gran – but with Mum? Come on!

Mum asked if I wanted to join in, which was so obviously a completely lame question she must have meant it sarcastically. I didn't even bother to answer and went up to my room and locked my door. There was no reason to, but it felt so good to be able to.

When I went into the bathroom later I nearly choked. Luke had put up a Post-it note of his own above the loo, just like mine. Idiot. Typical of him to copy me.

In fact, he'd put two huge ones up because he'd practically written an essay!

THERE ARE 12 STEPS DOWN AND
4 AVERAGE-LENGTH STRIDES ACROSS
THE LANDING FROM MY ROOM TO REACH
THIS TOILET (WHERE YOU ARE READING
THIS), COMPARED TO ANOTHER 12 STEPS,
(MAKING A TOTAL OF 24 STEPS) PLUS
6 AVERAGE-LENGTH STRIDES (MAKING
A TOTAL OF 10 STRIDES) TO REACH THE
DOWNSTAIRS TOILET.

THEREFORE I HEREBY INFORM ALL
CONCERNED (THAT'S YOU, TABITHA)
THAT I WILL BE USING THIS TOILET
WHENSOEVER I REQUIRE.

Ooh, I could strangle him, the little know-it-all. 'Whensoever I require?' 'I hereby inform?' Had he swallowed a dictionary before he wrote it or something? Stuck-up nerdy-pants. Honestly!

I took the notes down straight away, of course.

I might not be able to stop him using the same loo as me, but I'm not going to leave his cretinous notes up, am I? There was a real reason for my note. It was necessary because of him not aiming his disgusting wee correctly. My note had serious, proper instructions that he needs to follow for everyone else's sake. It wasn't a joke. His notes are just some stupid imitation of mine, and obviously only put there to annoy me. I'm not going to let him know the notes *did* annoy me of course – he'd love that. I'm not going to mention them at all. Hah! See how he likes that – all his 'whensoever, I hereby inform' lah-di-dah rubbish will just go completely ignored.

At supper Mum told me that Luke was going to go and see Dad for a few days over half-term and asked if I wanted to go too. Oh god, I wish she'd warned me before she'd made the announcement. I don't know what to do. Obviously I think about Dad and I miss him and everything, but I sort of don't want to go and stay with him because it's all changed now. I'm getting used to our new life here, without him but with Gran, Basil and, best of all, of course, Emz and A'isha.

If he's not here and we can't see him every day and can't have a normal life with a mum and a dad who live together and don't row the whole time, then I don't really want to have to think about him and deal with what he's like now and how he's changed because of the drinking. I am cross.

I was wondering what to say, when Gran gave me a really sweet smile and said, 'Why don't you think about it for a bit?' before I had a chance to say anything.

Mum was obviously annoyed with Gran for saying that. 'Thanks, Mother, I'll be the one dealing with him (she doesn't use Dad's name any more) if Tabitha ends up *not* going!'

Gran gave Mum one of those looks that means, 'I'm not going to say what I'm really thinking,' and then actually said, 'A little sensitivity, don't you think, Kat?' and then she turned to Basil, who was sitting on his back legs by Gran's chair with his paws up, waiting for the scraps she feeds him like he always does when we're eating (I don't know why she doesn't just get him his own chair so he can actually sit at the table with us) and said, 'Your sister's never been very sensitive, has she, Basil? Not like you, no, you are very sensitive, aren't you, my darling lad?' Then Gran replied, in her special Basil voice, 'Yes, Mummy, I am a very sensitive and caring doggie.'

It was hilarious. Mum looked like she was going to explode. 'God, Mother, you are so irritating. You do this on purpose to annoy me. I *am* sensitive! How could a dog possibly be more sensitive than me, a human?' Mum shouted at Gran.

Luke and I looked at each other and started laughing. It is so funny when Mum gets wound up by Gran.

To make matters worse, then Gran replied, 'I don't know, darling. That's a question only you can answer.'

Mum made a growling, angry sound and then said, 'Well, good luck getting Basil to push you around in your wheelchair when you're old and frail and can't take care of yourself!'

Luke and I nearly fell off our chairs we were laughing so hard.

'And I'm sure he will, won't you, sweetie? You can

push a wheelchair because you're a very clever doggie,' Gran said to Basil, giving him a big kiss – on the lips, yuck, mankenstein. I love Basil but kissing a dog on the lips – come on, vom-making-city.

'Oh, you're impossible!' Mum said, as she picked up her plate and marched over to the sink. Gran then gave Luke and me a naughty look, like she was asking us 'Did you enjoy that?'

I do feel a bit sorry for Mum when Gran pits Basil against her. I'm sure Gran does love Mum more than her dog but she also enjoys winding Mum up, which is a bit silly for a grown-up woman who is a granny. I know I like winding Mum up but she's my mum and I'm a teenager – that is what I'm supposed to do. I wouldn't be normal if I didn't. Sometimes Gran seems more like another teenage daughter than Mum's mum.

I guess I will think about going to see Dad, but I wish I didn't have to. It would be nice to see him and maybe he'll be a bit better and a bit more together and maybe not drinking. I hope so.

SUMMER TERM WEEK 4

FRIDAY

Today's the day I'm going to Emz's house after school – I cannot wait! I just had a fight with Mum at breakfast about getting back from there, though. She tried to insist she was coming to pick me up! There is NO WAY Mum is coming round to Emz's and maybe meeting her parents. I would literally rather die!

I just know Mum would be super embarrassing and would wear something awful from a second-hand shop or, as bad, start talking about her blog and maybe even suggest they read it, or she'd talk about splitting up with Dad. Whatever she'd do, say or wear she would, for sure, totally and definitely have embarrassed me to death.

I mean, to start with, we don't even have a car any more, so that would mean Mum walking up to their house and, if it was cold, probably wearing one of those stupid hats Gran's knitted for her with a pom-pom on top. Can you imagine anything more embarrassing than your own mother wearing a pom-pom hat? Oh, wait a minute, yes, I can – your mum wearing one and walking a dog wearing a matching one! And Mum probably would have told Emz's parents that she'd had to walk because her 'ex' had lost all our money, blah, blah, blah, and now we couldn't even afford a car. Oh god, I can't even bear to think about it.

Eventually I told Mum that I just wouldn't go to Emz's at all if she didn't let me walk back with A'isha. I told her that A'isha lives in those flats round the back, not that far from us, which isn't completely true, but we could walk a bit of the way home together. In the end, good old Gran persuaded Mum I'd be fine and reminded her that she used to walk back home from her mates' when she was my age.

I am not a baby. I am thirteen years old – nearly a grown-up. As I keep saying, in some countries I could be married with children by this age. Bleurgh, yuck, puke, what a disgusting idea, though — but you know what I mean. If it's okay to have a husband at my age somewhere in the world, then I think it should be okay to walk home not too late at night.

♡FRIENDS♡

Just back from Emz's house. So much to tell, but first of all, guess what? Guess who I saw walking back? Yes, Snap-Dog Boy! I left Emz's just before nine o' clock. Mum had made me promise I'd be back by nine for some reason. Yeah, because, like, obviously murderers and muggers and people who are just generally evil all keep a really tight schedule and never go out until after nine!

A'isha had to leave earlier — her dad had said she couldn't stay after seven and had come to pick her up, which I think was really mean of him. But she said she was lucky he'd let her come at all as he doesn't usually let her go to people's houses, and then only if he's met their parents or been to their house first. She joked that it's all part of his Messed-up Muslim rules, so I guess it was good she got to be there for a bit. After she'd gone, Emz and me did a bit more Googling and watched a bit of TV, but it wasn't as much fun as when all three of us were together.

I walked home, it's pretty much the same way I go with Basil when I take him out, but it's a tiny bit further. I am NOT going to tell Mum, but it was actually a bit scary, especially without Basil. I didn't see anyone creepy but I just felt a bit, I don't know, alone, I suppose. It was getting a bit dark, obviously, and there weren't very many people around and I just kept thinking someone was going to jump out of a bush or something. They didn't, but it did feel very nice when I got home and Gran answered the door.

Anyway, I saw HIM in the same place as last time, just at the top of the main road. Snap-Dog Boy was coming towards me with his dog. I saw him before he saw me, which meant I had time to think about what to say. I started walking really slowly so I had more time. As I got close to him I sort of smiled, but only a bit, you know, not like a crazy smile, like I'm his biggest fan or anything. I didn't want to look too like, 'Oh, hello, I've been dreaming about bumping into you again for ages and talking about it with my two best friends!' Just an ordinary smile like you'd give to someone from a different class to yours at school who you don't know that well – that sort of smile. Not a full smile, more of a half smile, you know?

At first he gave me a blank look and then, thank god, said, 'Oh, I didn't recognise you without your dog!'

I laughed, a bit too loudly I think, and then we both just stood there, not saying anything, which was really embarrassing.

I wish I'd had Basil with me. Then I could easily have thought up a dog-related question! But I was so pleased to see him again and it was absolutely brilliant that he remembered me.

I'll take Basil out tomorrow. Hope I see Snap-Dog Boy again. I must think up a couple of good, casual things to say, casually, and practise them first, too, so they don't sound all rehearsed and like I've thought about them for ages, which I will have done, obvs, but *he* mustn't realise that.

DOG QUESTIONS

It was great at Emz's. Her house isn't as massive as I thought it would be, but it was really lovely. Practically everything was white, even the floor. We had to take our shoes off the nanosecond we got in the door. Thank god I didn't have Basil with me – he'd have wrecked the place in about two minutes. There were white sofas in the living room, and all the walls were white, too. Emz said we weren't allowed in the living room. She was obviously a bit embarrassed about that, so I didn't say anything, but I did think it was a bit weird.

The three of us went into the kitchen. That was all white, too – not one scrap of any other colour. You couldn't even see the fridge or cooker – everything was behind white cupboards, which looked like the walls.

It turned out her parents weren't there. Her mum had left a note and a few snacks out for us – crisps and a pizza (only one!) and stuff like that – which I guess was nice of her but it did feel a bit weird and sad that there was no one there, especially as Emz is an only child.

I could tell Emz minded because she said, out of nowhere, 'Mum and Dad are never in when I get back. Actually they're hardly ever here at any time. I don't care!' But I think she does.

After we'd eaten all of the snacks (I was still hungry but I didn't want to say anything in case I made Emz feel bad and I didn't want to seem like a pig), Emz went and got her laptop. It's a really swanky one and looked nearly new. She didn't say anything about it and she wasn't at all show-offy. She might not have parents who are ever around but she does get things like that instead. Not bad, I say.

We mucked about for a bit, Googling random stuff. Then I had an idea. I felt a bit bad but sort of wanted to make sure we all had a really good time together at Emz's house, I guess, so that neither of them could go away thinking it had been a bit boring and it had been a mistake to have had me over there as well, instead of just the two of them. A'isha would obviously have been there loads of times before I came to HAC . . . So, I suggested we look at my mum's blog for a laugh.

Oh man, even though it was my own mum, and I suppose it was a bit mean of me, it was so worth it! Mum's blog is all about me, and how badly behaved I am and how I never do anything and never help and how I always side with Gran and Basil (!!!) against her. It was hilarious.

Emz and A'isha were killing themselves laughing! At first they thought Basil was my brother or uncle and I had to explain to them that he was a dog, and about Gran always putting Basil up against Mum, and how Gran treats him like he's her child. They couldn't believe my mum – a grown-up woman (well, sort of) – was jealous of a dog!

The best bit was that they both said their mums complained about exactly the same things (though not the Basil stuff, obvs). I was really relieved to hear that because, while we were reading it, I suddenly panicked that they might think Mum was right and change their opinions of me.

And then A'isha, who is always a bit less sensible than Emz, suggested we 'join in the discussion', which basically means we type a comment pretending to be normal readers of Mum's blog – a fed-up mum with kids like her. At first Emz thought we shouldn't, but then she gave in.

We came up with a brilliant fake name – WhydoIalwaysdoeverything? We chose that because it's what my mum says all the time and it turns out so do Emz's and A'isha's! Also, it seemed a lot like all the other mums' names on the blog, which were all a bit moany – like PutuponMum and QuickerifIdoitmyself.

Personally, I think you should be much nicer and kinder to your daughter, we (or rather WhydoIalwaysdoeverything?) wrote, *and buy her more things that will definitely make her happier, like her own computer and an iPhone, and iPad, and give her a TV for her own room, as well. If you do all that she might be nicer to you.*

We couldn't stop laughing once we'd sent it. But then it all went a bit wrong and I wished we hadn't done it, because Mum posted back, almost immediately, and completely spilt her guts, saying she couldn't do any of that because she was really poor and that her marriage had broken up because her husband was an alcoholic and had spent all the money they'd had and she'd had to move in with her own mother.

Oh god, I wanted to die of shame. I pressed quit as quickly as I could, but I knew Emz and A'isha had already read what Mum had said.

There was a really awks silence for a bit and then I said I was going to go, but Emz said, 'Tab, don't go . . .' and she looked at A'isha and then back at me. 'We don't care what your mum said or if your dad's a . . . you know . . . Or if you live in your granny's house. You're our mate. It's been a brilliant since you came to HAC.'

A'isha was nodding really hard. 'We three are BFFs and that's what matters. Don't worry about all that – who cares?' Emz said, nodding her head towards the laptop.

I nearly cried. I wanted to hug them both but I thought that might look really mad. I could have burst with happiness – my best mates now know the truth about how I've come to HAC and it doesn't make a bit of difference to them. Best result ever!

SUMMER TERM
WEEK 5

FRIDAY

This whole week, I've felt on top of the world, like it must feel when you're a pop star or a movie star — everything's great and everyone likes you. Obviously not like, 'Get me, I'm so beautiful and thin and everyone wants to be me' — just the inside-feelings those people probably have most of the time!

We had that supply teacher again, the one who'd made me sit on my own. This time, I was ready. I'd already worked out a plan for when we had her again, and I'd been sitting on the plan until we did. I couldn't wait to put it into action.

She walked in and, as usual, I was sitting at a table

with Emz and A'isha. As soon as she was in the room, she paused at her table and immediately looked at me. She didn't say anything. She just gave me a you-know-what-I'm-going-to-say look, her eyes wide open, eyebrows raised way up high and her lips tightened up, pinched together like a hen's bottom.

Part one of my plan: I just smiled back, really cheerily, like I was super pleased to see her again. After I'd done that for a few seconds I raised one of my hands and gave her a little wave, like it was just so golly-gosh-super-exciting that she was back.

Emz and A'isha were giggling by now, but Miss didn't notice. She looked like thunder and blurted out, 'Tabitha Baird! You know what I want!'

Part two of my plan: act totally and completely like I don't. 'No, Miss, I don't. How could I?'

Oooh, that made her cross. She stomped round to the front of her desk and pointed at the empty table she'd made me sit at the last time. 'Sit here!' she barked.

I gave her a sort of I-don't-understand look, and then stood up very slowly. I walked towards the table and could just tell the rest of the class was waiting for me to say something, which is exactly what I'd hoped.

Time for part three of my plan: 'I don't mind sitting here, but I don't know how I was supposed to know what you were thinking. I mean, we've only met once before . . .' I said as I sat down. I put on an upset expression and carried on, 'It's not like I'm a mind-reader, or anything, Miss.'

The whole class burst out laughing. Absolutely everyone. It was fantastic.

And then – the bit I had prayed would happen, happened. I had just prayed and prayed she'd say what Mum always says. Miss half screamed, 'I have just about had enough of you, Tabitha Baird. Just get on with your work!'

She'd said exactly what I needed her to say.

I got my pencil case and books and stuff out and gave her just long enough to get back to her desk and sit down and then, very slowly, I put my hand up. The whole class's eyes were on me.

'What?' she asked. She was obviously close to properly losing it.

'Miss? Can you let me know when you've *actually*

had enough of me, please?' I said, very politely and calmly.

A few of the class sniggered, obviously having worked out what I was saying. They were quicker off the mark than Miss, though, who clearly didn't have a clue what I meant.

'What on earth are you talking about, Tabitha?' she asked crossly.

'Oh, I'm sorry, let me explain. A minute ago you said, "I have just about had enough of you, Tabitha Baird". So, you know, I'm just asking if you could let me know when you've *actually* had enough of me, if that's okay, Miss? That'd be great.' I really drew out the word 'actually', so it sounded like 'aakshuuulleeeeee'.

Miss looked confused and just stood there with her mouth open – not a good look, especially if you're trying to control a class that's already laughing.

I decided I could keep going a little bit before she completely exploded. 'You see, Miss, when you say to someone, "I have *just about* had enough of you," there's a big difference between that and, "I have *actually* had enough of you," and I was just asking if you wouldn't mind letting me know when you'd got to the "actually had enough of me" stage.' (Again, I said actually like 'aakshuuulleeeeee'.)

Oh man, Miss looked as if she was literally going to blow up right there and then. And the whole class was laughing.

And then the very best, most unbelievable thing in the whole world happened. Miss turned around and stormed out of the class! I am not lying. She walked out of our class! My cheek had made a teacher leave the class. Result. Look, okay, I did think it was a bit extra and, well, kind of worrying. I mean to make a teacher walk out is quite a big deal, but what could I do once she'd done it?!

Everyone turned to look at me.

I could see some people's expressions were a bit worried, so I smiled, shrugged my shoulders and said, 'What did I say?' and everyone broke into more laughter.

That has got to be one of the best moments of my life so far. It's definitely the best day of my life at HAC, that's for sure.

As I was leaving school, word had obviously got round about what had happened and people I didn't even know were giving me looks like they respected my courage, as if they were noticing me for the first time — and in a good way. I mean, it's not very often you can annoy a teacher so much they actually walk out of class, is it? I've never even heard of a teacher storming out of a class before. And I had got one to do it! Pretty amazing, eh?

When I got home I came up here to my room, just to chill and think about my brilliant day. I lay on my bed and stuck my hand down the side to find Muzzy, and do you know what that horrible little worm, Luke, had done? He'd stuck a Post-it note on poor Muzzy's head! He had actually stuck something on my favourite toy's head!

I could stick *his* head down the toilet he insists on using, even though he still can't aim his disgusting wee into it. I will definitely aim his head into it properly, that's for sure. I am so cross. Luke has ruined my brilliant, brilliant day with his cruel and completely stupid Post-it note. And what he'd written on it wasn't

even funny. It was just, like him — totally moronic,
pathetic and lame.

PLEASE DO NOT STUFF ME DOWN THE
SIDE OF YOUR BED. I AM NOT A PILLOW.
I AM YOUR FAVOURITE TOY CAT. I
AM HAVING TROUBLE WRITING THIS
BECAUSE OF THE INJURIES CAUSED BY
YOU STUFFING ME DOWN THE SIDE OF
YOUR BED. GOODBYE.

I am so going to get him back for this. And it means
he's been in my room, the little rat! I'm going to have
to set a brilliant trap for the next time he comes in.
I don't know what yet, but it will have to be something
stupendous. Must think of something super clever.

Just as a precaution, I won't put Muzzy back there
because even though she didn't actually write that note
(if she had she wouldn't have posted it on to her own
head, no one would) she might, in real life, not like
it down there, between the side of my bed and the
wall. Not that I will ever in, like, a gazillion years, be
admitting that to Luke.

SUMMER TERM WEEK 5

SATURDAY

It's Saturday. I'm bored. I made the mistake of saying I was bored in front of Mum who then, of course, helpfully suggested I do some homework, clear up my room (so original, Mum) or, get this, clean the oven! She's so funny! I nearly fell over laughing. Not.

Gran said she'll get a DVD for tonight so that we can all have a meal and watch something together, but that's hardly the most exciting, glamorous thing I could do on a Saturday night, is it? I should be at a party or on a date with Snap-Dog Boy. Okay, perhaps not a date, that's a bit . . . I don't know . . . mature and yucky, but you know, we could go for a walk or get a coffee or something else not too datey and obvious.

I don't know how grown-ups actually agree to go on dates with each other. Talk about laying your cards all out on the table. If two people who like each other make a date to have dinner or go to the cinema or whatever, it must be so completely obvious to both of them that they are really saying 'I fancy you' that they might as well not beat around the bush and just admit that they only want to do whatever it is they've agreed to do because they fancy each other. Then they wouldn't have to bother with the whole date thing – unless they were hungry, I guess, or really wanted to see that particular film.

But, I mean, how incredibly embarrassing it would be to arrange a date when both of you know what you're really saying is, 'I want to snog you, but I'm pretending I want to have supper with you or see some film with you.'

Oh man, I'm never going to go on a date-date, not like a proper, official date. I'll just say something really cool and straightforward to whoever. Typical of grown ups to have invented some super complicated roundabout way of avoiding saying, 'I like you'. I'll bet me and my mates never do anything like that.

Gran's just brought up a letter for me. She said it had only arrived that minute. It's from Dad. I can tell from the handwriting on the envelope. Gran must have realised it was from Dad, too, because she put it on my table and then left the room, shutting the door behind her.

I've never had a letter from Dad. Who gets letters from their dad? Who gets letters from anyone these days? Dads don't write letters, except when they're in prison, I guess.

I'm not sure I want to read it. What if he says stuff about missing me? Or, more like, what if he *doesn't* say anything about missing me? What if it's all jolly and talking about what a great time he's having living at his mum's? Oh god, what if he asks me how Mum is? I really don't want to have to think about any of this. I wish he hadn't written at all. I'm going to take Basil for a walk. I might read it later. Huh. I'm cross.

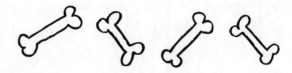

When I offered to walk Basil, Gran was thrilled. 'Oh, that's terrific, it'll give him a chance to wear his smart new coat – he's going to love it, it's so cosy and warm.' Then she pulled out an actual knitted coat-cardigan thing with sleeves – four obviously. Gran had sewn buttons on it as well, to make it look just like a coat or cardigan, but you couldn't undo them, so, really, it looked like a tube with four littler tubes (for his legs) coming off it. As if that wasn't bad enough, it was pink with little bones all over it! Pink?! Basil is a boy. It's bad enough that he has to wear these things – Gran might at least knit them in boy colours!

'It's not cold enough for that, Gran,' I said, desperately hoping she wasn't going to really put him in it. 'It's May!'

'Oh yes it is, Tab, and I want to wear it.' Oh god, Gran was doing Basil's voice. 'And it doesn't look just cosy and warm, it looks very smart too.' Gran was forcing the last of Basil's legs (I nearly said arms!) into the final sleeve. 'Oh yes, I like this, thank you, Mummy,'

Gran said as Basil. Yeah, like he'd be thanking her for that pink . . . coatigan thing!

To me, Basil did not look as if he liked it one bit. And he did not look smart. He looked completely bonkers. Or rather he looked like he belonged to someone completely bonkers who had forced him to wear it. If dogs *could* choose what they wore then no dog would choose this!

As soon as we were out of the door and round the corner I tried to get Basil out of his stupid new outfit. Seeing as I was the one walking him, obvs anyone would think *I* had put him in this stupid coatigan, and that it was me who was completely off my head. But he kept wriggling and barking and jumping out of my arms. He was driving me mad.

It turns out it's really hard to get a dog out of a tight-fitting knitted tube. In the end Basil literally leapt out of my arms and started running up the road at full speed with his lead trailing behind him. You'd think the knitted tube might have slowed him down, but not one bit.

I ran as fast as I could after him, but didn't manage to catch him until we were nearly at Emz's road. I ended up sort of jumping in the air, like I was doing a belly-flop off a diving board, and throwing myself longways on to the ground desperately trying to grab Basil's lead.

And then guess who, *of course*, comes round the corner just in time to see me lying on the ground wrestling with Basil while his lead is wrapped six times around my neck? The best look ever.

'Oh, natty coat,' Snap-Dog Boy said, as he helped me up off the ground. 'Knit it yourself, did you?'

I quickly unravelled myself from Basil's lead. 'Oh no, he's not mine – he's my gran's dog. She likes to dress him up and has conversations with him. She even has a special voice she does for him!'

As soon as I'd said it I realised it sounded like I thought this was a perfectly normal relationship for anyone to have with a dog. I'd meant to say something that would make it absolutely clear that I am not the sort of person who knits outfits for pets, but I hadn't wanted to be horrible about Gran either.

'What's it like?' he asked. I didn't know what he was talking about. 'The voice your granny does for her dog. How does it go?'

He was smiling in a non-sneering sort of way, so I realised he wasn't being nasty.

'I dunno,' I replied, shrugging my shoulders.

There was no way I was about to do Gran's Basil voice.

'Is it low and growly or squeaky and high?' he asked, looking down at Basil.

He was joking, I could tell, but there was still no way I was doing the voice.

'Looking at him, especially in that jaunty outfit, I reckon it's low and growly,' he went on.

I laughed out loud when he said that, because he obviously meant the exact opposite. Although I've always thought Gran's Basil voice should be low and growly too, he looked so ridiculous and silly in this particular outfit that if he DID have a voice it would definitely be a squeaky, high one to go with his coat-igan – just like the one Gran does do for Basil.

'So, I'm Sam,' Snap-Dog Boy said in a ludicrously low, growly voice. 'And this is my dog's voice. I've never tried it out before – what do you think? Her name is Bonnie, she's a girl, although this voice I'm doing for her does sound a bit like a boy-dog's, doesn't it? And my accent is Scottish because I'm a Westie, like your dog, and all Westie's are Scottish, och aye the noo.'

It was hilarious, his voice was going up and down. I couldn't stop laughing.

'What's your name?' he then asked in the same voice.

'I'm Tabitha, everyone calls me Tab,' I eventually managed to get out.

And then I couldn't think of anything else to say. I just sort of stood there because I suddenly felt a bit silly that I'd laughed so much, as if I'd never heard anything even remotely funny ever in my life before. I know that's probably a bit stupid of me but I'd laughed really hard, and I think a bit loudly, and I didn't want him to think that what he'd said was the first hilarious thing I'd ever heard. That wouldn't make me look like someone with a very interesting, jam-packed life, would it?

And then, before he said anything else, his dog pulled on its lead really hard and started whimpering and Sam said, 'Oh, sorry, that means Bonnie needs the loo badly. I'd better go, bye,' and off he went, waving a plastic poo-bag.

And that was that! No arrangement to meet again. No . . . no . . . I don't know . . . no nothing, just, 'Bye'.

I'd thought that once we'd actually spoken, we'd . . . erm . . . we could . . . we'd . . . oh, I don't know . . . well, just that it would all be completely different.

I'll walk Basil again tomorrow, and keep my fingers super-crossed that I'll see him then. And, by the way, Basil will NOT be wearing anything knitted. That is for sure.

The coatigan was pretty bad but, I guess, at least Basil didn't do a poo this time! That would have just been too much – can you imagine? Actually, I don't think Basil would have been able to do a poo wearing the coatigan – must tell Gran and then I'll never have to take him out in it again. Result!

SUMMER TERM
WEEK 6

MONDAY

Gran made a really delicious bread and butter pudding last night (with butter AND cream, *sooooo* yummy) and handed me a bit in a completely normal way, you know, because normal people make food, including puddings, and then offer them to the people they have made that food for, yeah?

Oh, but of course, silly me, that is in the normal world where people aren't completely controlling and crazy, like my mum.

My mad, controlling mum, of course, couldn't help herself and when Gran passed me the bowl Mum made her I'm-in-terrible-pain face and sighed loudly making it clear she disapproved.

I wish Mum wouldn't do things like that. It drives me mad. And it makes me feel so angry and bad about myself, the way I look and stuff. It's like every single time I eat anything that isn't a celery stick or a dry cracker or something revolting, Mum is on my case telling me not to eat whatever it is in case I get fat. And I just know she means fat-*ter*.

It's like she's judging me the whole time. Like I'm some sort of idiot who doesn't know how to eat. And the joke is that, with Mum breathing down my neck and watching me every time I'm even near the kitchen, I actually end up *wanting* to eat more than if she just left me alone! I know I wouldn't eat loads of biscuits and stuff if Mum wasn't always prowling around trying to catch me out.

Gran noticed Mum's sigh and expression. 'Leave her alone, Kat, she's fine,' she said.

'Hah, well, it's exactly what you used to do to me, Mum, when I was her age! You were always going on at me not to eat this or that!' Mum replied, sounding a bit like a teenager . . . A bit like me, I guess – and Mum's forty-one. Practically a pensioner!

Gran, as usual, replied in exactly the way she knew would be most likely to make Mum lose it. 'Yes, darling, and look at you now – lovely and slim – so my cunning plan obviously worked!'

'Well then, it will work for Tabitha too, then, won't it?' Mum practically screamed at Gran who, of course, answered straight back.

'No, because you're not as good at it as I was. Tab's just going to feel controlled and bullied by you, aren't you, Tab?'

Gran was smiling and doing this on purpose to wind Mum up, I could tell. And it was working, like it always does. I couldn't help feeling a little bit sorry for Mum having her own mum always teasing her. But I am really glad Gran's not joining in with the whole, Oh-Tab-please-don't-eat-pudding/biscuits-etc-etc nagging that Mum always does.

Oh yes, and by the way, she NEVER, EVER does this with Luke because he is, of course, her favourite and is also a stick-skinny runt. But still, she should be like this to both of us or neither of us. Unless, of course, she actually wants me to have proper proof, once and for all, that she loves Luke more than she loves me. Maybe she would love me as much as him if I never ate a single thing and ended up disgustingly, mankenstein-thin like Luke, who looks like a broom handle with a wig on top.

LUKE

So I read Dad's letter in the end. I didn't want to but I was bored so I thought I might as well. It's not like I was dying to see what it said or anything. And I wish I hadn't because it made me cry – only a bit, but still.

I know he's a bit hopeless and not very good at earning a living, or being a husband, or doing any of the stuff that grown-ups, especially grown-ups with kids, i.e. parents, are supposed to do, but the letter made me miss him and that's what made me cry. I don't want to miss him.

Way back (oh man, it seems like years but it's only months really), when Mum told us that we were moving to Gran's because we couldn't afford to live in Ivy House any more, and that Dad wouldn't be coming with us, I was upset that everything was going to change. But I didn't really think what it would be like to live without Dad. I don't know why. There was so much else to think about, I suppose. Luke had burst into tears, and after a bit I'd started crying too. Luke's crying had made me cry, I suppose, but it was also because of the news, obvs. Dad wasn't even there when Mum told us. He told Luke and me later that he 'couldn't face it'. Typical.

Anyway, in his letter Dad said he misses me and wants to see me and why don't I ever text him? It's not like he texts me that much! I suppose I could go and see him for a few days. It might be all right. At least he won't go on about biscuits and puddings and all the stuff I shouldn't (according to Mum) be eating.

Urgh, I just went on Facebook and Grace is trying to be my friend! I don't know what to do. Obviously I'm not going to accept. Everyone would think she *is* one of my friends. Hello?! I don't think so. But you can tell when someone's rejected your friend request. And even if I don't reject it and just ignore it for a bit, that will *look* like a rejection. It would definitely feel like a rejection to me. I never ask anyone to be my friend on Facebook, it's just so desperate.

I checked out Grace's page and she actually says that she goes to homework club! I mean, who puts that on their profile? You might as well put, *I am the UNCOOLEST person in the world!* She put that she's in the debating club at school too! I wouldn't put that either, although, I admit, that is a fraction better than saying you're in homework club, which is, literally, the worst. Grace has got twenty-seven friends on her page but some of them look like they must be relatives, so it's not like she's really got twenty-seven actual, proper friends. I've got a hundred and six, and most are real friends . . . Okay, not real-life friends who I've actually met but, you know, people whose stuff I like.

I suppose I could accept her because it is good to have loads and loads of friends on there, making me look super popular, and if you've got tons of friends then no one's probably going to notice a few Grace-types amongst them. It's not like anyone's going to go through your entire list of friends, unless you're, like, madly in love with someone, I s'pose.

Hmm, still don't know, though — it is a bit risky. If I accept her she might start joining us at lunch, or worse, try to sit with us on our table in class. She is quite brainy, so that would mean I could copy her answers and stuff, but I don't know whether that's worth the risk of actually accepting her as a friend. I'm going to leave it for a bit, and see what she's like at school and if she says anything about it.

I did walk Basil, even though it was rainy and wet, mainly because I wanted to accidentally-on-purpose bump into Sam, as I now know Snap-Dog Boy is called.

Sam, Sam, Sam. Good name, isn't it? I like that name and it goes so well with Tab, doesn't it? It's THE perfect name to go with mine. Sam and Tab. Tab and Sam. Tabitha and Sam. Tabitha and Samuel (I suppose he is a Samuel? All Sams are Samuels, aren't they?) Samuel and Tabitha. Urgh, no, Samuel and Tabitha sounds like something out of the Bible. Sam and Tab or Tab and Sam – those sound the best and really cool, too.

But I didn't see him! I don't know why. I walked Basil around the usual time I usually see Sam and his dog. I'm so annoyed – I got wet and cold and stayed out much longer than I would normally, just waiting to see if Sam turned up, in case he was a bit late taking his dog out or something. It was nearly an hour before I ended up going home. An hour walking round in the rain?

I hope Sam wasn't round a corner watching me wait so long – how pathetic would that have looked? Basil thought it was Christmas! He obviously couldn't get over his luck at being allowed to run about for so much longer than normal. He kept scampering about and then stopping for a bit and looking up at me like he was going to say (if he could speak, which everyone, apart from Gran, knows he actually cannot because he is not human!), 'Really? Can I keep running around? Are we really staying out this long?'

It was quite sweet, actually, but I won't be doing it again – sorry Basil. Hanging about in the rain on the off-chance that a boy I hardly know turns up is not a good look.

It was quite sunny and warm today, so during lunch break A'isha suggested that we all climb onto the roof of the art annex to sunbathe. It's the perfect place because the roof is completely flat.

The art annex is a sort of Portakabin bungalow thing. At my old school this was exactly the same type of thing the builders used as their temporary tearoom/store cupboard while they were building the new performance wing and here, at HAC, it's used as an actual permanent classroom! Still, I'd much rather be here, even without posh buildings for every single department. Who cares about that?

The roof is super easy to get onto actually – you just climb up a big tree that grows at the back and then jump across from the top branch. I guess it's a bit dangerous, if you're chicken, which I'm so not. You are definitely not supposed to go up there but you'd have to be an idiot not to be able to make that jump.

The best thing is you can't be seen from the main playground unless someone is actually looking right up at the roof. So, once we'd got up there we all rolled our skirts up and tucked them into our knickers so that we'd tan our legs properly. A'isha was wearing tights so she had to take them off first. 'Dad makes me wear them no matter how hot it is, for modesty,' she said, doing a silly face and laughing. And she took off her hijab, too. 'It's not like he's ever going to find out, is it?' she said as she scrunched it up and stuffed it into her bag. And then Emz and A'isha rolled the waistbands of their skirts down too and squished them into the tops of their knickers. There was so much skirt material all puffed out from the tops and bottoms of their knickers it looked like they were wearing nappies! I nearly died laughing.

'What? Why are you laughing? We'll get brownest this way. We'll get the most tanned we can get without going nudie-rudie!' A'isha yelled at me. I didn't say it out loud but I had thought she might not be that bothered about tanning cos of being mixed-race but she said she wants to get her legs as brown as poss.

Neither of them could see how funny it was until I said they both looked like they'd done a huge poo, which they did. Then they split their sides laughing.

It was really hot up there. We kept looking down at the playground and watching what everyone was doing. It was great because no one knew we were watching them. I spotted Grace, wearing her skirt, as per usual, the way it's supposed to be worn, i.e. regulation-for-nerds-only length. Even though that's how she always wears it, it looked even more ridiculous than usual in the hot weather.

I was just about to point her out to the other two when I realised she was on her own and I felt bad, so I didn't. I don't know why I feel sorry for Grace, but I do. I wish I didn't. Just like I wish I didn't feel sorry for Dad, either.

And then, you will not believe this, Grace looked

up and saw me and waved! I am not kidding – she waved at me! And not just a small wave of her hand, oh no, not Grace – it was a full-on massive, whole-arm-and-hand wave, like she was bringing in a plane. So, of course, what happened? Obviously one of the teachers, who was on playground duty, noticed Grace waving like a loon. The teacher goes over to her and looks up in the direction Grace was waving and sees – who else – me, of course! Thanks a lot, Grace.

The teacher, Ms Dryden (usually known as Ms Drippy-Dry. She teaches maths and there are no laughs in her classes ever) marched over to the hut. Emz and A'isha had already started wriggling backwards away from the edge of the roof on their tummies, like they do in the army, to stay flat and out of sight. If they'd stood up, Miss would definitely have seen them as well. It was too late for me – I knew she'd already seen me.

Emz and A'isha were whispering, 'Ouch, ouch,' because the roof was scratchy. We already knew that because of lying on it, but I guess it's scratchier if you're slithering along it on your bare skin, like a worm.

'Shhh,' I hissed at them, 'we'll all get caught.'

'We're already caught, brainbox,' A'isha hissed back.

'You're not – it's only me so far,' I hissed just as Ms Drippy-Dry got there.

'Tabitha Baird, what a surprise. How did I know it would have to be you?' Ms Drippy-Dry shouted up, super sarcastic. 'Who is up there with you?'

I looked down. 'No one. I'm up here on my own.'

I could hear Emz and A'isha trying to stifle their giggles behind me.

'I don't believe that for one minute. You never do anything without an audience,' Ms Drippy-Dry said meanly, which made me instantly decide to annoy her.

So, instead of coming straight down, as she obviously expected me to, I stayed lying on my stomach and then rested my chin on my hands, all casual and relaxed, like it was a completely normal thing to be talking to a teacher while lying on the roof of a school building. 'I don't think that's fair, Miss Dryden,' I replied, acting like I was quite upset.

'Yes, it is. You're always showing off. You're in constant need of attention. I can't imagine you doing a single thing alone.'

'Hmm, well, that's not true. Let me think. Ooh, yes, I know, I go to the toilet all on my own!' I replied, making out like that was an amazing big deal and that I really thought it deserved her praise.

I quickly looked back. A'isha and Emz were literally stuffing their hands in their mouths to stop themselves laughing out loud.

'This is ridiculous. Get down here this minute and go straight to Miss Wright's office. This is a matter for the head teacher!' Ms Drippy-Dry snapped.

I'd obviously succeeded in really annoying her. Good. I was pleased. She deserved it. She shouldn't have called me a show-off. So what if I do always muck about to make people laugh – that's my thing. I don't think it means that there's anything wrong with me, does it? I hope it doesn't. Everyone likes someone who's a laugh. Don't they?

Ms Drippy-Dry marched me up to the head's office and went in first, making me wait outside. Mrs Bras gave me an oh-you-again look. I just ignored her and her stupid boobs, which is pretty hard to do because they are enormous and all over the shop.

When Ms Drippy-Dry came out she gave me an evil stare. She'd obviously told Miss Wright everything. Big deal.

But, oh my god, Miss Wight was much more furious than I'd expected. I thought she was going to have a heart attack. She went on and on about health and safety and how I could have been killed or seriously injured (she actually managed to make 'seriously injured' sound worse than being killed!). And then she blathered on about how she'd warned me that I was on notice, blah, blah, blah, and that I'd disappointed everyone by continuing to behave badly, blah, blah, blah, and that this was the last straw, blah, blah, blah.

I stopped listening. She just kept saying the same thing over and over again, only using different words, like grown-ups always do when they are telling you off and don't know when to stop.

'Are you taking any of this in?' I suddenly heard her say.

'Yes, Miss, of course I am,' I replied immediately,

although I hadn't heard a word she'd said since 'disappointed everyone'. I'd completely zoned out.

So, the first thing I *actually* heard her say after that was, 'Very well then. I'll be writing to your mother when I've made my decision.'

Now, obviously, I had no idea what she was talking about. Eh? What decision? I've got brilliant at pretending to listen over the years. She probably means some stupid detention or something. Obviously it's super-boring that she's writing to Mum because Mum will, of course, freak out and then write on her blog about how awful I am because I got a detention or whatever punishment Miss Wright has decided to give me for my huge, terrible, world-shattering crime. I don't care though – it's not as if Mum can do anything, really, can she? Apart from go on more about how I shouldn't eat biscuits! Big deal.

As I left the head's office I bumped straight into Grace in the corridor.

'Thanks a bunch, Grace. You waving at me got me caught! Drippy-Dry wouldn't have known I was up there if you hadn't waved at me! Miss Wright's just had a real go at me, all thanks to you.'

I wasn't actually that bothered, but I wanted to have a go at her because it *was* her fault that I got caught.

'I wasn't waving at you, Tab, honestly.'

'Yes you were, don't deny it. I saw you. You were waving all over the place, like a looney-tune. I'm surprised an aeroplane didn't land on you!'

'I promise I wasn't waving at you. A wasp was buzzing around me. I was trying to make it go away. That's why I was using both my arms. You must have seen – no one waves with two hands, do they?'

She had a point, I had to admit, but I didn't want to let her off the hook. 'Yeah, well, maybe, but I still got into trouble because of you,' I replied, after a bit.

Grace didn't say what I would have said if anyone had blamed me for something – she just said, 'I'm sorry about that!'

God, how pathetic. If the whole wasp story was true, then it definitely wasn't her fault, but she still said sorry!

I felt a bit bad for her, and that she was so willing to apologise when it wasn't actually her fault — according to her, that is.

♡FRIENDS♡

When I saw Emz and A'isha later they told me Ms Drippy-Dry had made them admit they'd been up there with me. A'isha was panicking a bit in case Ms Drippy-Dry told her dad she'd taken off her hijab. But, they said, she blamed me for it all because apparently I am 'a bad influence' on them! I was a bit upset about that, because it wasn't true that I'd made them go up there. In fact I had made sure they *didn't* get caught as well as me. I told them it was Grace's fault, really, that I'd got into trouble. I know that's not completely right but, you know, I wanted them to know that it hadn't been my fault that Ms Drippy-Dry had spotted me.

It felt quite cool that I had taken the blame for all three of us. It sort of makes me the leader of us, in a way, don't you think? Like I'm the daringest, the bravest, the most . . . I dunno, just the most, yeah?

SUMMER TERM WEEK 6

FRIDAY

It's the last day of school before half-term. Emz, A'isha and me have arranged to meet at the bus stop near school so we can all walk in together.

I'm going to suggest we always do this from now on when we go back after half-term. It's nice us all walking into school together, side by side. It's like we're saying, 'Here we are, check us out, the three coolest girls at school.'

I'm really, really, really going to miss them. I won't see them during half-term because I've decided I will go and see Dad. Luke is going anyway and I decided I'd better because I haven't seen him for weeks and it'll be nice (I hope) and also it'll be good to get away from Mum and all the don't-eat-this-or-that nagging for a bit

And it'll be quite good to have a break from walking Basil, although I suppose that means I won't see Sam for a week either. But then maybe he'll miss me. Obviously I don't mean 'miss me' big time, like we're a couple or something, but, you know, maybe he'll notice I'm not around and then wonder where I am . . . and think about me and stuff, and that'd be good.

Anyway, must go as I don't want to be late meeting up with Emz and A'isha.

SUMMER TERM
WEEK 6

SUNDAY

When Luke and I got off the train, Dad and GB were standing on the platform waiting for us.

I could not believe Dad had brought his mum! We hadn't seen him for nearly two months. Honestly, you'd think he might want to see us alone, even just for a few minutes.

I soon found out why he'd brought her, though. As we climbed into GB's car she said (in that sing-song voice that Mum says is her way of saying, 'Everything's lovely' even when it's not), 'I hope you don't mind your old gran coming along, but your poor daddy was so nervous about seeing you both after such a long time I thought I'd give him a little moral support.'

Luke and I were in the back and looked at each other. We were both obviously thinking the same thing, *Poor daddy?*

I admit Dad was never as do-y as Mum. It was always her organising everything. But GB was talking about him like he was an invalid who was going to face scary monsters or something, not his own kids!

Even though her house is quite big, GB put Luke and me in the same bedroom, which we were both annoyed about, though me more than him. I am *thirteen* years old! I can't believe she thinks I'm okay about sharing a bedroom with my ten-year-old brother. I'm way too grown up for that. There was no point in saying anything, though. She showed us to our room and in that same annoying voice said, 'Here you are, in together, just like when you were little. Aaw, won't that be lovely?'

With Gran I could have explained why it was not going to be lovely at all, but then Gran wouldn't have done it in the first place. GB seems to think Luke and I are still babies!

LUKE

We had a nice supper and it was good to see Dad. He didn't have anything to drink at dinner but neither did GB, so it was hard to tell if Dad's actually given up (like he always, always said to Mum he would) or doesn't drink in front of GB. Let's see if Dad keeps it up over the next few days. I don't want to be checking up on him, though – that isn't my job.

It used to feel like it was my job, though, because sometimes when they were together Mum would ask me if I'd seen Dad have a drink. I really hated that. I didn't want to lie to Mum, but I didn't want to have to watch everything my dad did. It made me feel like I was the grown-up – like they were my kids and I was supposed to look after *them*! I'll bet no other kid in the world feels like their parents are actually their kids.

SUMMER HALF-TERM

MONDAY

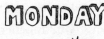

Dad asked us what we wanted to do while we were there and if we wanted to see any of our old school friends.

'Oh yes, definitely, that'd be brilliant!' Luke cried out.

I definitely *don't* want to see any of those girls from my old school, but I didn't say anything because I thought GB might go on about what a lovely school it was and what a shame I was now at a not-so-lovely school, which is what she thinks about HAC even though she knows absolutely nothing about it.

She thinks my old school is brilliant in every single way. It's private, so, for her, that makes it better than anywhere you don't pay for, anyway.

GB suggested we take a drive past our old house, but both Luke and I, together said no immediately.

'Oh, that's a shame. I'd love to see what the new people have done,' GB said. 'That house needed so much work – it could have been so beautiful. I always wondered why your mother didn't get round to organising it.'

Luke and me looked at each other. We both knew what she really meant – it was Mum's fault our old house had never got all done up, like hers, and that was the reason Dad had become a drinker.

I don't know why but I instantly felt like I had to stick up for Mum. 'Mum says she never really liked that house anyway,' I said, super-casually, like it was just a normal piece of information.

'Hmm, well that was pretty clear,' GB replied, sort of under her breath but deliberately-on-purpose not quite enough, i.e. we were supposed to hear it but she could pretend that she hadn't meant us to hear, which made me really cross. It's not Mum's fault. That house was enormous and Dad was the one who wanted to buy it but then hardly ever did any of the bits of fixing-up Mum asked him to do.

And then Dad said, 'I loved that house,' in an I-feel-so-sorry-for-myself voice.

'I know, darling, this has all been so hard for you,' GB sighed to Dad – in front of us two! Luke and I looked at each other, amazed. We could not believe what we were hearing! Dad's mother, our own grandmother, was actually saying, in front of us, how difficult it was for *him*.

'Mum said we should never have bought that house, it was far too . . . too,' and then, suddenly, I couldn't remember the word Mum had used.

I was furious. I wanted GB to stop blaming Mum for everything. I knew this word explained why she didn't like the house, in a way that didn't blame anybody.

'Isometric!' I said, desperately hoping that was the word. 'Yes, Mum says the house was too isometric,' I repeated.

GB narrowed her eyes and made a sneery face like I'd just farted really loudly or something.

Maybe it wasn't 'isometric'. I didn't know for sure but I wasn't about to admit that in front of her.

Luke looked at me and whispered, super quietly,

'You mean isolated. That's what Mum says — it was too isolated, like far away from everything. Isometric means three-dimensional.'

For once, I was really grateful for Luke's swottiness. I knew he was trying to make sure no one else heard. Luckily, they didn't.

'ISOLATED!' I practically shouted out, 'That house was too isolated, that's what Mum thinks,' I continued, quite loudly, sort of trying to cover up that I'd got the word wrong the first time.

'Well, it was a bit, I suppose,' Dad said, at last.

'Hmm,' GB said. 'Something like that is only ever a problem if you make it one!'

Luke and I stared at each other. We knew exactly what she meant — everything that had gone wrong was all Mum's fault.

SUMMER HALF-TERM

TUESDAY

I'm not going to tell him but actually it was quite fun sharing a room with Luke. It meant we could talk which was really nice. We talked for ages. We haven't done that for a long time.

We decided that GB had never liked Mum (which is what Mum had always said anyway) and that actually probably no one in the world would be good enough for her little boy – our dad!

Luke asked about HAC and if he'd like it there. I told him it was great and much more fun than my old snooty school.

Luke told me he liked his new school better than his old one too and actually quite liked living at Gran's but that he missed Dad a lot 'even if he is a bit hopeless at being a grown-up.'

I didn't say I did as well, because although I do, I thought I might cry if I said it out loud and then Luke might take the mick or, worse, start crying too.

Anyway, I think Luke probably misses Dad in a different way to me – more like a boy missing a dad to do boy-type things together, even though Dad didn't ever do many of those either. Dad wasn't very do-y around the house or with us.

I'm beginning to realise that Dad just isn't a very do-y type of person – maybe that's why he drinks. Maybe he wishes he was more do-y but just doesn't know how to be. There must be some real reason why people drink too much. It can't just be so that they can get out of doing stuff.

Just as we were going to sleep Luke started imitating GB's voice which gave me the giggles.

'Oh darling, don't be horrid to your poor old daddy, he's only forty-six years old. It's not his fault, nothing is his fault, he's only little, my darling boy.'

Luke does her voice really well.

'You know,' I said, just before I fell asleep, 'Gran says the same sort of things about Basil.'

Luke nearly died laughing.

SUMMER HALF-TERM

WEDNESDAY

Oh my god, I don't know what to do. I feel sick. Oh god, oh god, oh god, I'm so upset. I literally don't know what to do . . . or think!

When I went downstairs this morning, Dad was on the phone. I could hear it was Mum because she was shouting, but I couldn't hear what she was saying.

Dad was just standing in the hall with the phone pressed to his ear and his shoulders all slumped, like a kid who was being told off. I couldn't work out what was going on. Then I heard him mumble into the phone, 'What am I supposed to do about it? It's not my fault.'

When Dad spotted me he said, 'She's up now. Why

don't you talk to her?' and handed the phone to me. Obviously Mum hadn't agreed because as I took the phone she was shouting, 'I don't want to talk to her, I am so angry – why don't *you* tell her?'

'Hello, Mum, it's me. Dad's gone,' I said, trying not to sound as nervous as I felt.

'Yes, I'll bet he has. Typical, he doesn't want to deal with yet another disaster!' Mum shouted.

'Don't have a go at me. I haven't done anything!' I hissed back.

'Yes you have!' Mum screamed down the phone. And then she told me what she was ringing about.

Oh god, oh god, oh god. Rats. Bums. Grrrrrr. Apparently the letter that Miss Wright had said she was going to write to Mum 'letting her know her decision' had arrived this morning and she has given me a whole month's worth of detentions! One entire month! That is so over the top. Oh god, I think I'm going to throw up. Apparently she considers me climbing on the roof to be very serious because not only did I endanger my own life, but that of two other pupils. If it wasn't because I had just started at the school and she realised I was obviously finding it very difficult to settle down, she would have considered suspending me – and if anything like this happens in the future she will! Miss Wright said that when she talked to me, I didn't appear to be very sorry, or understand just how easily I could have had a serious accident.

It's not really, actually my fault I hadn't been 'very sorry' cos I hadn't been listening when she was talking! I might have been 'very sorry' if she'd bothered to tell me that's what she wanted me to be!

Mum was going absolutely bonkers. She kept shouting and yelling down the phone.

I started crying, not because Mum was shouting at me – she's done that loads of times, although, I admit, this was the worst I'd ever heard her – but because I realised I wouldn't be able to hang out with Emz and A'isha every day after school. It was such a long time! It was making me really upset. What if they stopped liking me because I wasn't around any more? What if someone else took my place? What if they just completely forgot about me? A whole month of not being able to hang with them after school is a complete disaster!

Mum said the letter went on about my 'bad

behaviour' and that Emz and A'isha's parents were very upset about the bad influence I appeared to have on their daughters, making them go up on the roof and risking their lives, and encouraging A'isha to take off her hijab and disrespect her faith. It was so incredibly unfair – that was nothing to do with me!

'I didn't *make* them go up on the roof! We all did it – it wasn't just me!' I screamed back at Mum. It was so unfair. I'll bet Emz and A'isha didn't really say it was all my fault. It wasn't even my idea in the first place – it was A'isha's. I'm not saying it was all her fault either, I'm just saying it wasn't my idea alone. It wasn't like I forced them up there against their will.

I was so angry and upset. I started sobbing and Mum started crying too and then shouting at me again.

Suddenly GB appeared from nowhere and just took the phone out of my hand.

'Go into the kitchen, have some breakfast and calm down, please,' she said bossily.

I was grateful she'd taken over because I'd got so upset I could hardly speak and Mum wasn't making much sense by then either. I know they don't really like each other much, but I hoped that maybe GB would make Mum see that perhaps it could all be sorted out.

When I went into the kitchen Dad was standing by the sink drinking coffee and looking down into his cup, all sad and hopeless. He looked up at me when I walked in and shrugged his shoulders and then I saw an open bottle of whisky behind him. He hadn't even tried to hide it.

I wanted to kick him. He shouldn't have been feeling sorry for himself and he definitely shouldn't be drinking. This is supposed to be when he, my dad, is supposed to know what to do!

'Why are you drinking, you crappy loser?' I screamed at him. I couldn't help myself. I couldn't believe that the first thing he did as soon as there was any trouble – some actual parent stuff for him to do – was to start drinking.

'Don't have a go at me, darling. I don't know

what to do. What do you think I should do?' he moaned.

I just lost it. 'Why are you asking me? I'm not a grown-up, *you* are, or you're supposed to be. That is your job as my parent!'

'It doesn't look like I'm very good at being one though, does it?'

'You're not even trying!' I shouted at him. 'At least Mum is taking care of us and trying to manage. You're asking me to be grown-up for you!'

Dad didn't say anything and then GB walked into the room. She looked at the whisky bottle and then at Dad, but she didn't tell him off. I doubt GB has ever told Dad off for anything in his whole life. No wonder he thinks he can do whatever he likes!

'Right, that's all sorted then,' GB said, looking pleased with herself. 'I've made your mother see sense, Tabitha. She didn't like it at first, but she realised I was right. You're going to stay here with your father and me and go back to your old school. Clearly this new school you're attending hasn't got the faintest idea of how to properly manage or educate a young girl.'

What? Are you joking? Are you having a laugh? My head

was spinning but I was dumbstruck. I couldn't speak.

I couldn't believe they'd do this to me. I couldn't believe Mum would leave me here. I couldn't believe Mum would let GB keep me. I didn't know what to say. I was reeling. I thought I was going to be sick.

Dad broke the silence. 'I can't afford the fees, Mum.'

'I know, darling. Don't worry, I'll sort all that out,' GB said to Dad, as if a grown man being broke and not able to take care of his own kids was a completely normal thing.

Neither of them even looked at me. It was like they thought this whole mammoth decision had nothing to do with me, like it was just up to them.

'There is no way I am going back to my old school and even more no way I am going to live here with you two!' I shouted really loudly. I didn't care what either of them thought by now. 'You can't make decisions for me!' I said crossly to GB.

'I am your grandmother and as such —'

I wasn't going to listen to this rubbish. 'Dad can't even make decisions for himself, never mind anyone else. But you are not going to control me too!'

I stormed out and ran upstairs to my room. Luke

wasn't around. I didn't know where he was, but I knew I couldn't hang around waiting for him. They weren't going to force me back into that school. And they were not going to make me live with them.

I wanted to talk to Muzzy but I'd left her back at home. She was on top of my bed – not stuffed down the side. Not because of Luke's stupid Post-it note, though – just because . . . I don't know, just because. She looked much happier there. But I wished I'd brought her with me.

I stuffed all my things into my rucksack and pulled my shoes on. I couldn't really think what to do next. My head was pounding and I felt shaky and I sort of wanted to cry, but I knew I couldn't, not now – there was no time for that.

And then I heard Dad at the door. 'Tabitha, darling, can we talk? Please don't be cross with me.'

I didn't reply. I couldn't think what to say.

He just hasn't got a clue — not a single clue.

Then I heard GB say to Dad, 'Leave her be. She'll come down when she's hungry,' and that did it. I was so angry that she obviously just thought I was having some sort of babyish tantrum. This is my life! This is the most important thing that has ever happened to me in my whole life ever and she thinks I'll forget about everything when I want something to eat!

I decided I had to get back to London. I had to find a way to sort everything out.

SUMMER HALF-TERM

WEDNESDAY
(LATE MORNING)

I opened the window, leant out and looked down at the garden. It was a pretty big drop but I didn't think it was big enough to break a leg or anything. There was no other way out without risking GB or Dad seeing me, so I had to go out of the window. There was nothing else for it.

I felt bad leaving Luke behind, but he's only ten – I couldn't take him with me. And anyway, he had no reason to leave. They're not making him live with them, like a prisoner, and forcing him back to his old school. Still, he probably won't want to be here all on his own.

But I am not hanging around. I left a note for him. I didn't say where I was going, though, because although

I'm pretty sure I could trust him not to tell on me, I bet they'd make him. I don't want them to know – they'll just try and find me and force me to come back here and I am never coming back, never, ever, ever.

I lowered my rucksack out of the window first, using the fancy ropes GB has round her curtains to hold them neatly in place when they're open. She will *not* like that.

Good. I don't care. Then I got out onto the ledge. Looking down I did suddenly feel that the ground was miles away, but I knew I had to escape. So I sort of wriggled my whole body around to face the inside of the room and then lowered myself down, hanging on to the ledge, getting my feet just a bit closer to the ground and then I panicked, I looked down and the ground seemed just as many miles away as before. I felt sick and wobbly – I wished I could just climb back in and pretend none of this had happened but it had, and there was no way I was going back to Greyfriars and super-no-way I was living with GB, so I closed my eyes and just let go. There was nothing for it, unless, of course, I wanted to deal with GB finding me casually dangling out of the window, like it was the most normal thing in the world to do.

In the end it was okay. I hurt my ankle, which meant I had to hobble instead of walk properly, but at least I was down. I ran as best as I could to the bushes that edge GB's garden and crawled under them in case Dad or GB came out and spotted me.

I got all the way to the gate on my hands and knees, dragging my rucksack and clambering through the bushes. I got covered in dead leaves and yucky bits of garden stuff – completely mankenstein. I looked like a scarecrow by the time I got to the road and could finally stand up. It wasn't a great look, but luckily no one was there to see me.

I started walking, or rather hobbling because my ankle had got quite sore, towards the village. I planned to get a bus from there to the train station. Luckily I had kept my return train ticket in my rucksack and I had five pounds that Gran had given me. It was just over a mile to the village but after a bit I realised it was going to take ages because of my ankle. I couldn't go back. I didn't know what to do.

And then I saw Jim – GB's gardener – coming towards me in his truck. I panicked. What if he told GB or Dad he'd seen me?

He slowed down and called out of the window, 'Hello, Tabitha, your granny told me you were coming down for half-term. What are you doing out on the lane lugging that big rucksack? You look like you've been dragged through a hedge backwards.' He thought he was very funny.

I had to make something up quick. 'I've been . . . I've been . . . I'm going . . . Orient– orient– ?' I said desperately. I couldn't think of the word for pointlessly going around the countryside for ages using only a map to find your way.

'Orienteering?' Jim said helpfully.

'Yes, I've been doing that! Got all my . . . erm . . . maps . . . compasses and things in my rucksack, I've got to meet up with the other . . . erm . . .'

'Ah, so are you meeting up in the village?' Jim asked.

'Yes, I'm meeting other . . .' What were they called? 'Erm, the other orienteerer-ers. I'd better go,' I said hurriedly. The longer I stood here chatting with him the more chance there was of everyone realising I'd gone and come after me.

'Why don't I give you a lift there? It'll only take a minute. You can save your energy for the rest of your orienteering. You'll need it,' Jim said cheerily.

I didn't reply. I just jumped straight into his truck. I was so grateful I didn't have to keep walking on my bad ankle.

There was a bus already waiting in the village, which was brilliant. Plus, extra brilliant, when I got my fiver out to pay, the driver said he didn't have any change and smiled and told me not to worry about it. I was so pleased.

I hadn't had any breakfast, or anything to eat at all' in fact, since last night. I was starving. I planned on getting something at the train station but there were no shops. There was not even a kiosk at that station — not even a guard.

I got a bit nervous waiting in case Dad and GB turned up, but I didn't think they'd have worked out what I'd done in time to catch me before I got on the train.

I took out my mobile and saw I had a missed call from GB's house. Jim had probably told them he'd given me a lift and about my fake orient. . . whatever it's called, plans for the day. I don't think GB or Dad would believe for one second that I'd gone on a big, long hike (I never did that sort of thing even when we lived in the country). GB will just decide I'm sulking. But they probably won't realise I've actually run away. Well, not yet, anyway. And by the time they do, no one will be able to find me. All the same, I was super relieved when I'd got on the train and it pulled away.

After a bit I decided I actually had to tell someone I'd run away, you know, to make it official and A Real Thing, not just some hissy fit, so I sent Mum a text: *Because of you letting GB take over I have run away. You will never, ever see me again for the rest of your whole entire life. I hope you are sorry now. Goodbye forever.*

And I didn't even put a x. Then I switched off my phone.

Mum is going to be so sorry now!

A grotty old cheese sandwich and a yuckily tepid Coke from the trolley on the train used up the whole of my five pounds! That was all I had in the world. I literally did not have one single penny left but I was so starving there was no choice. The sandwich was bone dry and tasted like someone had been sitting on it all morning. It was completely and totally mankenstein but I ate it, obvs.

I started to think about what had happened. I'd got so angry with GB and Dad and then caught up with running away, I hadn't really had time to think about Miss Wright's letter.

As the train chugged along, it all began to sink in. I couldn't believe it. Miss Wright had actually given me a whole month's detention and threatened to suspend me! A whole month? That is equivalent to torture. No one gets a whole month. A whole week, okay, maybe, if it's like major, but a month?! Apart from expelling me it is about the worst thing she could do, and all just for being up on a stupid roof that wasn't even *that* high off the ground. Well, I suppose it was *quite* high, but we def wouldn't have died even if we had fallen off it, which we weren't going to do, obvs. She should see the window I'd just jumped out of. Actually that probably wasn't quite as high, but then I didn't really hurt myself. Okay, so I did hurt my ankle a bit, but it's not like I actually broke anything. Anyway, it is so pathetic and lame of her. And *sooooooo* extra.

I don't think I deserve to be given such a long detention time. It's really, really, really super-unfair of Miss Wright. And she hasn't even given me a chance to tell my side of the story.

It's all that moron Grace's fault for waving at me. Ms Drippy-Dry would never have seen me if she hadn't done that. I don't believe that wasp story. I am going to kill her. Oh god, I can't believe this. I don't think it's fair at all. I love my new school.

Obvs, I don't love the schooly bit, but I love it *there*. I love my friends and how different my life is now and how different *I* am there.

I fit in at HAC. I never really fitted in at Greyfriars.

HAC just feels right, like I belong there. I don't want to sit inside with some boring teacher for one whole month! I am going to miss so much. And I'm so worried everyone will forget about me.

I mean, I realise I haven't been, like, a brilliant student, or most likely to be voted head prefect (as if I'd want that anyway – can you imagine anything more pathetic and losery?), but I don't think I've been bad enough to deserve this. It is so unfair. I wish I knew what to do. What if everyone forgets me?

SUMMER HALF-TERM

WEDNESDAY (LATER)

When the train got in to London – the final stop – everyone started gathering up their stuff and getting off. I was the last one to leave. There was no hurry because I realised I hadn't made a plan, other than running away. I didn't know where to go or what to do next. But I wasn't scared – I just didn't know what to do really.

Okay, I was scared a bit and, you know, I wanted to go back to Gran's, but I couldn't. Mum obviously doesn't want me around any more. I mean, she'd never have agreed to let Dad keep me if she did, would she? I know Mum and I row a bit and I s'pose I'm a bit mean to her sometimes, but she's my mum. Mums aren't supposed to kick their kids out. It wasn't my fault I'd got into trouble. And anyway, kicking me out is a bit extra – leaving me in the country with Dad just because of a bit of detention!

I knew when Mum found out I'd run away she'd get really upset and blame herself. Good. She'd be right to blame herself. It *is* her fault. I'd never have run away if Mum hadn't *given* me away to Dad and GB. I mean, god, she could hardly bear Dad's mum when she and Dad were together, but now suddenly she thinks it's okay to force *me* to live with her!

I hope Mum is really, really worried about me.

Everyone must know by now that I've run away. Good. That'll teach them for making decisions about me without asking what I want first.

I switched my mobile on and saw that I had six missed calls from GB's house and eleven missed calls and five texts from Mum. Eleven calls! I'd only run away just over six hours ago and Mum had already called me eleven times. I know I'd switched my phone off but I wouldn't have answered her calls anyway.

I have run away and I am not going to tell anyone where I am. I want them to be frightened and worried about me. Bonus – Mum will probably regret ever going on at me about eating biscuits and stuff, too. GB is really going to regret trying to make me go back to my old school. And I hope Dad is going to regret starting drinking again. Serves them all right.

I hobbled over to a bench in the station and sat down. I needed a bit of time to try to work out what to do next. I literally didn't know what I was going to do. It dawned on me that when you run away you should, first of all, have a plan. And, most of all, you should definitely make sure you've got some money with you. And probably some food too. But I hadn't had time to do a detailed running-away plan had I? It's not like I'd had masses of time to set up a whole running-away project complete with instructions, illustrations and handy tips!

While I was sitting on this stupid bench wondering what on earth I was going to do with the rest of my life now that I was officially A Runaway, I suddenly got a huge whiff of a horrible, mankenstein, stench. I looked up and saw a hunched-over old man wearing the dirtiest coat I'd ever seen in my life, standing literally about an inch away from me. His coat was tied together with bits of old rope and all the way round his waist, hanging off the rope, were about a million ancient plastic bags filled with other plastic bags. The smell coming off him made me want to vom.

'Spare us some change,' the man said, stretching out a completely black-with-dirt hand.

'I haven't got any money,' I replied crossly. I couldn't believe he was begging money off me. I was a runaway, couldn't he tell?!

I didn't want this stinky old man talking to me. But he didn't go away. He just stood there not saying anything. I didn't know what to do.

'Not even the price of a cup of tea?' he eventually mumbled.

'I don't have a single penny in the whole world and I'm hungry too!' I replied, trying really hard to fight back the tears by now.

He didn't say anything – he just stood there.

And then he put his grime-covered hand into his

pocket and whispered, 'Here you go,' and handed me a fifty-pence piece. 'Take care of yourself.'

And he shuffled off really noisily because his shoes were made of plastic bags done up with elastic bands.

And then I did cry. I was frightened and alone and I didn't know what to do. I didn't know where to go. And a smelly man who couldn't even afford shoes had been nice to me and given me fifty pence.

'Tab? Is that you? Are you okay?' I heard someone ask a few minutes later.

I looked up and you will not believe who it was. It was Grace. Grace was standing in front of me.

'Grace, what are you doing here?' I asked, quickly wiping away my tears. I did not want her to see me crying.

'I've been visiting my . . . erm . . . auntie. My mum's just coming to pick me up. Do you want a lift? Mum won't mind,' Grace said.

I didn't know what to do. Of course I didn't want

to stay the night on the bench in the train station, but I couldn't go home. I had nowhere to go.

'I've got a month's worth of detention for going up on that roof. Miss says if I don't improve she'll suspend me and my mum's kicked me out,' I blurted. It just all came tumbling out of my mouth.

'Oh dear,' Grace said. She paused for a second, then said, 'Why don't you come back to mine then?'

I've never been to her house, obvs – we're not even friends. Oh god, and I'd never even accepted her Facebook friends request. Here she was being so nice to me and coming to my rescue and everything and I hadn't even been that nice to her. I felt really bad about everything now.

'Erm, okay, thanks, but, erm, do you mind not telling your mum about it all . . . yet, please. Is that okay?' I asked as we walked out of the station. My ankle was really sore but I hoped Grace didn't notice.

'Yeah, fine, whatever,' Grace replied. She was being so cool and casual, like what I'd just told her wasn't that big a deal at all. Her being like that made me feel much calmer.

Just as her mum arrived I heard my phone ping. It was yet another text from Mum.

Darling, please, please, please let me know where you are and that you are okay. I am going out of my mind with worry. I love you with all my heart. xxxx

Tears sprung into my eyes. I felt a bit bad for her. She sounded really upset. But then I felt angry again. If she loved me with all her heart she shouldn't have agreed for me to move into GB's house miles away, should she? I felt all jumbled up inside.

I turned my phone off and decided I'd think about it all later.

Grace's mum was like a bigger version of Grace. She was even wearing a hairband and a cardigan with all the buttons done up, though not a school uniform one, obvs. But she was really nice and just seemed to think it was super normal for Grace to bring someone she'd just bumped into back to theirs.

Their house was really nice and cosy. It looked quite

a lot like Gran's house inside, which made me think of Mum and Gran and Basil and I felt all sad again.

I was absolutely starving and super relieved when, as soon as we got in, Grace's mum told us she'd already made supper. 'So, Tab's staying over tonight, Mum, okay?' Grace said to her mum but looking at me, just as we were finishing eating.

'Fine, if it's okay with your mum,' Grace's mum said smiling at me. She was so nice and friendly and laid back, like nothing was a surprise or a problem.

'Yeah, it is, thanks very much,' I replied.

Grace grinned at me and gave me a little thumbs-up under the table so her mum wouldn't see. I hadn't decided yet if I was going to let Mum know I was okay. I wanted her to worry for as long as possible so that she'd really, really regret what she'd done and never do it again.

'Did your mum really kick you out?' Grace asked, while we were clearing up. Her mum had gone out to meet some mates. There was no dad around as far as I could tell.

I don't know why, but it made me feel good that Grace's mum was a single parent, too, like my mum. I realised we were more like each other than I'd thought before. Because of the hairband and the way she wears her school uniform and being a swot and in homework club and all that stuff, I'd just thought Grace was so completely the opposite of me. She still is, but not so incredibly different, deep down, I guess.

Grace got out some nice biscuits for pudding – her mum had made them. I had three and Grace didn't say anything. It felt good to just eat however many I wanted without having Mum tell me not to.

Then I told Grace the whole story. It was such a relief to get it off my chest. Grace was brilliant and didn't interrupt once – she just listened until I'd finished. Grace was really shocked at what Miss Wright had done and how crazy Mum had got about it. 'It's not like you killed someone!' she said. Quite right – that *would* deserve a month's worth of detentions, I agree.

'I know!' I said. I was so pleased that even a goody two-shoes like Grace didn't think what I'd done deserved the punishment I'd got.

'I'm so sorry you got into trouble, but you know, I really didn't wave at you up on the roof. There really was a wasp,' Grace suddenly said. 'I really was trying to shoo it away. I got stung, look.' And then she showed me a little mark on her arm.

I felt terrible for thinking she'd made the wasp up – the sting must've been quite bad for there to still be a mark. It had practically disappeared, but it was there. It had seemed like such a fake story and so made-up-to-cover-her-crazy-waving, but I guess sometimes things happen that sound like they're made up but actually turn out not to be.

'Sorry,' I said.

'S'all right, it isn't itching any more,' Grace replied. And then she gave me a serious look and said, 'You know, your mum's going to be really worried. It's quite late.'

'Do you want me to go?' I said immediately, almost before she'd finished speaking. I wanted to stay. I liked being here with Grace. I like the way I don't have to try as hard with her – I can just sort of chill. But I thought she was maybe telling me to go.

'No, no, I want you to stay. I just think you should send your mum a text so she knows you aren't lying strangled in a ditch somewhere.'

I laughed. I know I shouldn't have, but that is *exactly* what Mum would imagine had happened. So, I sent her this text:

I am okay don't worry but I'm not going to live with GB and Dad. I am not going back to my old school no matter what you say.

And then I switched my phone off again. I knew Mum would ring the second she saw the text. I just wanted to be able to work out what I was going to do tomorrow and make sure I didn't have to leave school.

SUMMER HALF-TERM
THURSDAY

Grace and me stayed up practically all night chatting. It was really good fun even though I was pretty tired.

It turns out that Grace has never had a dad at all – literally, no dad! Her mum is gay, or rather, her mums are gay – they split up when she was little. She told me the auntie she said she'd been to see wasn't really her auntie – it was her other mum!

Grace said that she'd thought it would be a bit complicated to explain on the spot at the station that she had one mum outside waiting for her in the car and that she'd just been visiting a different mum! Two mums? How cool is that? No wonder Grace doesn't try hard to be cool – she's got the coolest family in the world, the coolest parents in the world! Two mums! Amazing!

I felt so relaxed and easy with Grace that I also told her about Emz's and A'isha's parents complaining to the school about me 'making them go up on the roof' and about A'isha's dad blaming me for her taking her hijab off. I told her I was worried that maybe they'd decided to blame me so they didn't get into trouble.

'I bet you a million quid they didn't. You three are so close, I can't believe they'd have done that,' Grace said. 'I reckon their parents just assumed they must have been forced to do something risky like that,' Grace continued. 'But you did tell everybody that you'd suggested it, didn't you?'

Did I? Well, I know Ms Drippy-Dry had leapt to conclusions and I'd been quite happy that she had.

'Yeah, well, I guess I was sort of pleased to be seen as the leader,' I replied. I couldn't believe I was confiding in Grace like this. 'Serves me right – look what's ended up happening to me because of it!' I said.

'Hmm . . .' Grace said. She was obviously planning something. 'I'm sure you'll be able to convince your mum to let you stay at HAC. No mum wants their child to be unhappy. And Emz and A'isha are obviously the key to getting you out of your month's detentions. We've got to get hold of them.'

I was worried that if I went to either of their houses their parents might not let me in. Because of everything that had happened, they obviously thought I had corrupted their daughters. I was also a bit worried that, whatever Grace had said, maybe they *had* told their parents that it was all my fault. I know that's a bit of a random idea but I didn't know what to think, really.

Grace suggested that she texted them for me. I wasn't at all sure that was a good idea. I was worried that if Emz and A'isha saw that Grace was sending a message for me they might think I'd suddenly become her bezzie and then not want to be mates with me any more because of that.

I didn't know what to do but I felt bad, too, in case Grace guessed that was what I was thinking.

But Grace was great. The next morning she just wrote them a text on my phone. *Hi this is Grace, on Tab's phone. She's been given a month's worth of detentions. We've got to think of a way to get her out of them, are you in?*

I was so nervous waiting for them to reply. It felt like years before they did. Suddenly my phone pinged twice in a row, really loudly. I nearly jumped out of my skin. Both Emz's and A'isha's texts basically said, *Yay! Deffo, let's meet up!*

Grace looked at me, smiling. 'Shall we arrange to meet them this afternoon, so you can go home and see your mum first? She's probably going to have completely lost it by now.'

I wanted to meet up with Emz and A'isha straightaway, but I knew Grace was right. Oh man, Grace is sensible – she even bandaged up my ankle this morning and it feels much better. I can walk on it pretty much normally. It's nice having a friend who knows what to do. Hmm, friend? Let's say, for now, Grace isn't my actual friend – that's a bit extra.

I'd barely got my key in the front door when Basil came shooting out of the kitchen at full speed, whizzing round the corner yapping and barking. I know dogs don't really smile, but I'd swear he did when he saw it was me. He shot up on to his back legs and jumped up at me, yapping and dancing about with excitement.

I scooped him up and gave him a cuddle. He was wearing a cape. I am not joking. Basil, the dog, was wearing an actual cape. Like a superhero wears but smaller and knitted. Superhero capes are never knitted. It was the worst thing Gran had ever made for him, but I didn't care. It was so good to see him.

Mum came out almost immediately after him, took one look at me and burst into tears. 'Oh, my darling girl, thank god you're home.'

I practically threw Basil onto the floor and ran to her. I was so pleased to see her.

'I'm so sorry, I just wasn't thinking straight,' Mum blurted out, squeezing me in her arms. 'GB steamed in with that plan and she was so sure it was the answer to everything and I'd just got that letter from school and I was panicking. I didn't know what to do. Oh, please forgive me, love. I was such an idiot. I thought maybe you really weren't settling and that you might be happier if you went back to Greyfriars.'

'I'm sorry, too, Mum. I didn't mean to worry you. I was just really cross. I am not living with GB and Dad!' I said.

'Of course you aren't. I'm just so glad you're home,' Mum said, all happy and cheerful. I hadn't seen her this chirpy in years. Oh man, she was so relieved I was home she seemed to forget to be angry with me for running away and making her so worried.

Result.

When Gran came in and saw me she actually squealed. Basil started yapping and doing a jig.

'Yes, isn't it wonderful, Mum?' Gran said in her Basil voice. 'It's so marvellous to have her home!'

I burst into laughter. Basil dancing and Gran doing his voice – it was all brilliant. I'd only been away from home a few days but the whole running-away-for-a-day thing had made it seem much, much longer. I do feel a bit guilty about worrying Mum and Gran so much, but a bit pleased, too, I must admit. It feels pretty amazing to know that just disappearing for not even a whole twenty-four hours can have that effect on people!

When it was time to go out and meet the girls I got worried that Mum might not let me go because of everything that had happened. So I thought I'd just pretend I was taking Basil for a walk.

'I'd really, really love that, Tab, thank you,' Gran said, using Basil's voice again. 'I've missed you.'

I think Gran really meant *she'd* missed me but was getting Basil to 'say' it for her.

Mum was on her computer and looked up suddenly. I could see she was worried. 'Tabitha, darling, you'll come straight home, won't you?'

'Yes, Mum, don't worry. Basil will drag me home!' I said, laughing.

'That's right, I will. I'm so pleased to have a chance to show off my lovely new cape,' Basil (Gran) said.

For once, Mum didn't even seem to mind Gran doing that.

'And when you're back we'll have the biscuits I made for you yesterday to distract myself, praying you'd be home soon,' Mum said giving Gran a quick look. Gran smiled back at her.

'Ooh, biscuits? You must have been worried,' I said. 'That'd be great, thanks.'

Mum gave me an I-know smile. It looked like she'd thought about a lot of things while I was 'missing'.

As I left the house I looked down at Basil in his ridiculous knitted neon-coloured cape trotting along beside me without a single clue just how much of a twit he looked. I thought about taking it off. I just knew the girls were going to split their sides when they saw him. But I didn't care – it's not like anyone's life is perfect. It was so great to be home. Now we just had to work out a way to get me out of those so ridiculously extra detentions.

Just before I got to the park near Emz's house, where we were meeting, guess what? I heard Sam call out from across the road.

I hadn't even noticed him. It was the first time in ages that I'd walked Basil and not thought about bumping into Snap-Dog Boy.

He was waving and it was pretty obvious he was going to cross over and chat. I did want to, but I didn't have time. I just thought, *I can't do this right now. I don't want to be late for my best mates. Sam, gorgeous as he is, is just going to have to wait.*

So I waved back and shouted, 'I've got to be somewhere. See you around.'

And, I have to say, he did look pretty disappointed! Oh yes! Result. How incredibly cool was that, and I hadn't even planned it?!

SUMMER HALF-TERM
THURSDAY
(LATER)

Emz, A'isha and Grace were already at the park, waiting for me. I could tell Grace was looking a little awkward with Emz and A'isha. I was so excited to see them I just ran towards them – well, as much as I could run on my ankle – screaming my head off.

Emz and A'isha jumped up and down on the wall they'd been sitting on and started screaming too. We made so much noise all screaming together! Basil started jumping up and down – he was loving it.

Thank god Grace didn't. It would have been superweird if she'd joined in, especially as I'd only just seen her that morning. And she isn't exactly our friend. Well, not yet.

'Oh my god, what is your dog wearing?' A'isha

suddenly yelled, pointing at Basil's cape which was flapping in the wind.

All three of them looked down at Basil. He was dancing about, superexcited, looking up at them with his tongue hanging out, like it always does when he's really happy. It was almost as if he was actually saying, 'I see you've noticed my brilliant cape!'

'Oh, that is *so* sweet,' Grace said.

'Sweet? Are you joking?' A'isha said. 'That is totally weird, man.'

'It's not weird, it's kinky,' Emz joined in.

'Oh, leave him alone, it's not his fault. Gran knits him outfits – don't ask me why!' I said, laughing.

It was so great to be back with them. And Basil didn't mind. It's not like he can understand. All he knew was that everyone was looking at him and laughing!

We all decided we needed to go somewhere where we could talk and then we realised because of Basil we couldn't go anywhere because most places don't allow dogs and even though he had his superhero cape to keep him safe and warm, I didn't feel happy about tying him up outside some café.

'Let's go to mine then,' Grace suddenly said.

Emz and A'isha looked at each other and then at me. The expressions on their faces were, 'What's going on? Do we really want to go to her house?'

But it's not like we could go to either of their houses, seeing as their parents apparently thought I was a bad influence, so I just said, 'Yeah, great, let's do that.'

Once we'd got there it was a bit all not-knowing-what-to-do-or-say. It was quite awkward and I was beginning to wonder if it had been a big mistake coming to Grace's.

And then Grace turned to Emz and A'isha and said, 'You two are probably wondering how on earth Tab and I suddenly seem to be mates and what that's all about.' Before going on she turned to me and said, 'Sorry, Tab, we are mates, now, yeah?'

I was so embarrassed. It was such an out-there question! I mean, who asks that kind of thing? It's so . . . so . . . I don't know . . . it's so extra. I didn't want to be horrible because she had really helped me, so I just mumbled 's'pose', and then Grace went on, 'So, Tab's been given a month's worth of detentions and Miss Wright says she's also going to consider suspending her if anything like that happens again.'

Emz and A'isha gasped. They hadn't properly known about the suspension bit.

'Mainly,' Grace went on, 'I think, Miss Wright's given Tab such a harsh punishment because it was dangerous – and especially because she thinks she made you two do something dangerous. So we've got to convince her that there was a real, proper reason for Tab being up there so that Miss will let her off the punishment.'

Honestly, it was like she was taking charge of a meeting or something. I felt a bit awkward and began to wonder if I really wanted to be matey with her. I liked her now that I knew her better but that didn't mean I wanted to hang out with a big swotty nerd or anything.

'But they know A'isha and me were up there as well,' Emz said.

'Yeah, so whatever pretend-real reason we come up with has to work for all three of us, because we got into trouble, too,' A'isha added.

'So, how come only Tab got the detentions?' Grace asked.

'Because Miss Wright thought I'd forced Emz and A'isha to go on the roof,' I said. 'And because their parents blamed me.'

'But why did their parents think that?' asked Grace, not letting it go. No wonder she was in the debating society.

I saw Emz and A'isha look at each other and then look away quickly. I knew they knew why. And then I knew that they knew that I knew why.

'Because you told them that, didn't you?' I said to Emz and A'isha.

I was quite cross and considering the detentions I think I had a right to be cross.

Emz and A'isha didn't say anything. They just looked at each other and then wouldn't look at me. I knew that it was true: to get themselves out of trouble with the head they had told their parents that I'd forced them up there.

I couldn't believe it. I was so upset. They hadn't stood up for me – they'd lied to save themselves.

'Oh my god, I can't believe you'd do that to me!' I shouted. 'That's the real reason I got into such trouble – because of your parents complaining about me. Look what you've done! I hate you!'

I dashed out of Grace's, only just remembering to take Basil with me. I ran all the way down the road.

I'd been so happy coming home and seeing Mum and Gran and Basil and my best mates and being back where I belonged. And now it was all ruined. It was all over – our friendship – everything was just completely and utterly hopeless. My two supposed-best friends had lied about me!

It was all so unfair! I didn't deserve this to happen to me. I had really, truly believed I'd made the bestest mates in the whole world, that the three of us were going to be best mates for ever and ever, that no one could ever break us up, that we'd always, always, always have each other. And now I'd found out Emz and A'isha obviously couldn't care less about me.

SUMMER TERM WEEK 7

MONDAY

The days before school started again were the worst of my whole life. I had no friends in the world and nothing to do. I did walk Basil but you can't really call him my friend. And I did talk to Muzzy but although I do love her a lot, it's not much good talking to a toy cat — just like Basil, she can't really say anything back.

MUZZY

Luke returned from Dad's. It was nice to see him but I'm not going to tell him that, obvs. He told me that GB had gone absolutely berserk when she realised I'd run away and that Dad had actually stood up to her and had said that he didn't blame me! GB will not have liked that.

Then today I had to go back to school and I wanted to die. I was so unhappy.

I didn't want to have to walk in with no mates and then stay behind afterwards for the first of seven thousand years of detention.

There was nothing for it, though. I had to go to school.

Just as I walked out of the door my phone pinged three times in a row.

All three texts said the same thing. They were from Emz, A'isha and Grace:

We've sorted it all out. It's going to be okay.

Can't wait to see you!

Xxxxxxxxxxxxxx000000000xxxxxxx

How could they have sorted it all out? What were they talking about?

I nearly collapsed, I ran so hard all the way to school. I had to slow down a bit just before I got there. I didn't want to go in all sweaty like a pig.

I arrived just before the bell went.

'Good of you to join us, Tabitha Baird,' Ms Cameron said sarcastically as I slipped in the door.

I wasn't even a whole minute late. I was just about to say something when I realised I'd better not. Maybe now wasn't the best time to start the backchat again . . .

Emz and A'isha were at our usual table and, get this, Grace was sitting with them too, like it was the totally regular and normal thing to do. They all waved at me to come over.

As I sat down, Ms Cameron gave us all a fierce glare like she was warning us not to start talking. We looked at each other and without speaking we could just tell that this wasn't the time to push our luck. But I wanted to explode, I was so desperate to hear what they'd done. I had to wait till break to find out.

It turns out that Grace, A'isha and Emz had come up with a plan. They went into school early today to see Miss Wright and their plan had worked!

It was really Grace who got me out of the detentions. She told Miss Wright it was actually her who'd asked us to go up on the roof to help her with a secret scientific experiment about shadows cast by the sun at different times of the day. There was some kind of national science prize she wanted to enter and Grace told Miss Wright that when she was doing all those hand movements we were recording where the shadows fell every time she waved her hand.

Thanks to her being a swotty nerd and never, ever having been in trouble before, not even once, Miss Wright completely believed the whole thing, including that we hadn't explained that at the time because Grace was desperate for the experiment to stay secret!

'And I really DIDN'T tell my parents it was your fault for making us go on the roof,' A'isha said. 'It was just when Miss Wright rang Dad up to say what had happened, she suggested you were really to blame and I let Dad believe it because I knew how cross he'd be. And then he decided you were to blame, for the whole hijab-thing too, and I have to admit I sort of let him. I'm sorry.'

'Same with me,' said Emz. 'My parents threatened to ground me over half-term, so I didn't say anything when Miss Wright said you'd been the ringleader. But I never thought only you'd be punished *instead* of us.

'We'd both felt really awful,' Emz went on. 'We were going to tell Miss Wright the truth and then Grace came up with her brilliant plan, so we didn't need to! And now, thanks to Grace, none of us have detentions!'

I wanted to cry I was so happy.

They'd done all this for me. I felt as if I could burst with happiness.

'So, am I now officially your friend?' Grace asked at lunchtime. Honestly, what a nerd. Who asks things like that? She is so extra. I was super glad Emz and A'isha weren't around to hear this – they'd have just died – and anyway I know her better and sort of get that she says moronic things like that.

'Yeah, okay, I guess you are, but FYI, cool people do not ask if they are people's friends. That is lesson one, okay?' I replied.

I really like her but she's going to have to learn not to keep saying lame things like that if she's going to hang around with me and Emz and A'isha.

'Maybe, but I don't want to be so cool that I end up being too cool for school. That's how you get a months' worth of detentions,' Grace said laughing.

I smiled because she was right. I was back where I belonged and I had to make sure I never got into that kind of trouble again. I had to find a way to keep being super-cool but not so cool I get into major trouble.

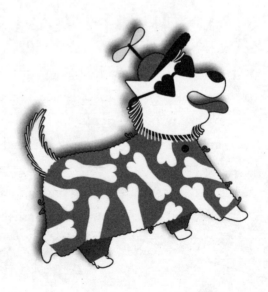

piccadillypress.co.uk/teen

Go online to discover:

☆ more authors you'll love

☆ competitions

☆ sneak peeks inside books

☆ fun activities and downloads

THE
ENDLESS TRIALS
OF TABITHA BAIRD

BY ARABELLA WEIR

Tabitha Baird and her friends Emz and A'isha reckon they're definitely the coolest, baddest and most popular girls in their year. Until new girl Ali arrives. She's so seriously goth, Tab calls her 'Dark Ali', and she doesn't like it, or Tab, at all.

At home Mum's blog is taking off and she's also got a new boyfriend (complete with a huge, not-trendy beard). But Mum's not the only one with a new love life - Gran's dog Basil is going to be a father and Gran wants custody of those puppies . . .